FISSION

PULP FACTION>60 ALEXANDER ROAD>LONDON N19 3PQ
distributor>central books (uk)>tower records (us)
http://www:tecc.co.uk/twin/pulpfact

First published 1996
by Pulp Faction
Copyright © Pulp Faction, 1996
Printed in England.
British Library CIP data: Fission
I. Palmer, Elaine
808.8'31 [FS]
ISBN: 1899571035

Editor:	Elaine Palmer
Assistant Editor:	Robyn Conway
Cover design:	Engine
Designers:	Michael Kowalski, Daniel Mogford, Martin Black.
Distributors UK:	Central Books 0181 986 4854
Website by:	Twin Media at http://www.tecc.co.uk/twin/pulpfact
Thanks to:	London Arts Board, the Paul Hamlyn Foundation and to all the writers and artists who have sent us their work.

Contents

text-flow

1

2   3

4 5 6

CCCCCCCCity

eroica mildmay

I've been invited out tonight. It's strange, I forgot that anyone remembered I was alive. As far as I knew, I was cubicled. Cubicle 18. The invitation is from somebody I worked for once, delivered a theory to. That's all I'm good for, the odd idea. Computers don't have any good ideas you see, no soul as yet. So we are one step ahead. They've cornered all the skills though. They've laid waste to us.

I don't have a job to speak of. What I do to survive, I never say. Leave it at that. This place is so small it makes you scratch just walking in here. But at least it's my itch. It's insane, but if you don't see people, just the touch of their skin can drive you wild, I mean peculiar. Just the concentrate of scent in a room full of people.

The town is very quiet tonight, mind you there are no open streets any more. They call it 'galleried', we call it 'compression'. We are compressed. Totally compressed. To think that now we realise that all we needed was space.

I must get ready. A muffled bang across town. It's probably a bomb. Another urban grumble, somebody-somewhere's cause. Everything, but everything is silenced, under the galleries. They are impenetrable. But no, it isn't just that, the place is dead, deadened. Even the planes, the only things permitted to be out of the gallerie structure, and in the unfit air, are silent as they whirl around this townscape, tipping this way and that as they square up to put down.

I need my Sector Pass, I put it down here somewhere. Without it you can't pass on the routains. You key in your journey, purpose, identity, and you pass only that way. Or, as they say, "you're free to travel on your designated route." Someone will always know where you are. Except, strangely enough, when you are still. If you stand totally, like Zen still, the system loses you. But then they key in the localised cornersite video and they've got you anyway. But I like keeping Zen still, it makes them work harder.

I'm nearly to the door. You know, I could still fall in love, I could take someone and inhale, enjoy and not judge. I could, I promise you, even though Ravetime news bombards the romance out of you, and comets are raining down on sister countries.

5

Something is going to happen tonight but I'm not sure what. Can't stop feeling weird. Some stupid accident on the routain is due to me perhaps. It happens, it moves along slowly, and if you're not concentrating . . . I might never get to the party. I hunch into the future.

Could I really fall in love? Unlikely. I don't even like people. Some of them are weird. A bit of plastic here, metal there, pig, dolphin, baboon, you don't know what you're getting. They are known as 'fittings' and I'm not keen, although you have to pretend to be tolerant. I've never had any surgery, I stay fit out of fear. The rumours are not pretty.

I can't decide what to wear so I don't change, I just stay stinking.

Well, I reason that a light barrier of scent will throw off all but the prince that I am seeking.

The lift parts like a pair of dry testy lips. It prickles horribly on the way down. Seriously hair-lifting static. In the foyer, the air is humming. I give it some thought. Everything you confront must be dealt with, that's what they say, but then they hate confrontation don't they?

It must be a routain engineer fuck-up – that tends to make the air bristle, everyone knows that.

I join a routain, everything is quiet. Through Sectors 3, 5 and 7, a quick unauthorised stop for a drink. The carton pops out so quickly that I don't run into 'idletime'. 'Idletime' gets the cameras really seeking you out, usually for removal or a talking to. Some people do it just for a talking to – to talk to people, anybody, even them.

The party is in Sector 8, somewhere through the silence. The world is built up to the teeth but so many of the people have gone. Where? Don't know. No one knows. We think there was a lot of killing. It became mad. War could be a glorious thing, that's what they said. They talked about it as a thing of beauty to offer your soul up for. Perhaps there was a war. Don't for a minute think I'm exaggerating. If you were not involved, you were ignorant and if you were involved you were dead. It's as simple as that. All you heard were stories. And that's why a party makes you want to weep, just the potential emotional release as much as anything.

I put my hand on the rail down into the Vault and 240 fucking volts rear up and rage through my system, scalloping out every single hollow in my body in less than a second. If I'd been a metal-part 'fittings' I would have sparked out for sure. Flesh is so much more forgiving. I pick myself off the floor and try to reconcile myself with my heartbeat which is skeetering all over the place.

My Pass clicks into Sector 8, and I turn into the routain where the party is. I pull my coat over my hand to press the Compartment button. Compartment 24. A fizz of electricity bubbles through the fabric, confirming that I would have probably got the full whack on bare skin. The video eye roves and settles on me like a grumpy chameleon. I am borne up to a distinctly better class of compartment than my humble cubicle.

My Sector Pass slices down the aluminium strip for the final frontier, and the door opens to reveal a room full of undulating bodies. How terrifying to see such humanity, such baseness. In a tidy, isolated world it takes your breath away. I move quickly to find a vital drink. Drinking to rampage through the evening, which I do. I talk to people and 'fittings' all night, and as prejudiced as I am to 'fittings' I laugh at all their jokes. I just wouldn't go to bed with them. It's a long shot but I'd hate to give birth to a piglet or something that had to live in water all its life.

The Vault feels very oppressive, unusually so. My chest remains tight. I don't touch a thing. The Vault runs under the river, it's always so damp, and now, lethal. I pass some people coming up in the opposite direction. One or two lights are out, and fuck me, don't they look ashen, but no one is complaining. But then no one does.

I stay late, very late, so I know now I'll wait until morning with the crowd. Get it whilst you can. And I certainly don't want to go under the Vault at this time of night. I shudder. There's plankton down there at nights, that's how low the low-life is. Even the authorities let it go, they just clear up in the morning. People get murdered and tidied away by those mysterious cleaners on the civic payroll. I grab another carton and let the liquid roll down my throat. Away with thought.

7

The party has a reckless feel, too much so. An unspeakable thing happens. The host opens the door to the balcony and the air beyond. Everybody gasps, and we, to a person, clutch at our throats. We mimic death, because we have been carefully schooled to anticipate it. It is forbidden to come into contact with the air beyond. Biblically so. It is dirty and lifeless. Only a 'fittings' with an evident brain bypass giggles. Baboon, you can tell, the slightly panicky chatter.

Open and die,

that's what they say
No laughing matter.

But we aren't dead, are we? The host is smiling and walking out onto the balcony like a dream. He leans calmly on the railing and gazes down on the miles of lit routains as if he was alone and dreaming. A few of us join him. The air is slightly particled. I have distant memories of the sugary grit of candy floss dissolving in my mouth. And perhaps it is a bit stale, but that is all.

I look across the townscape, the vast park areas, steamed up as always with cramped trees sweating against the glass. Above us a bullet plane wheels around, twinkling like a jewel. And far into the distance lies the airport, where you fly in to be clipped firmly onto a routain, so there too, you never come into contact with the air.

Our host sucks on the night air in the same way that he might pull on a cigar. He is unconcerned, we are unconcerned. But deep down you don't let go of fear so easily. I am worried for him, if the authorities knew they'd be down here like a flash. I wonder how many of these old-fashioned Compartments still exist that aren't fully modified to be airtight. Grand places like these have been preserved for posterity, and have always been given to the aware people who knew the rules. Our host is breaking them. Does he know something we don't? Doesn't he care anymore?

But what harm are we coming to? Someone pours a drink, in a subdued but civilised way. Catering staff at a funeral couldn't have done it better. The gravity of the rule-breaking is threatening to sober us up, and yet why? We are still here.

Below us I notice that a few lights are blowing in the routain network, leaving in some cases quite large sections unlit. I am glad not to be on my way home as Sector 5 is particularly badly hit. Someone comments on the amount of electricity they'd noticed in the air earlier and everyone nods.

We must have all had a prescience of some sort. I remember thinking that I probably wasn't going to fall in love that night, or ever for that matter. You need familiarity for love, not stale isolation. There is a nice looking 'fittings' for consideration, but for my unshifting plebeian wariness, and now, this awesome distraction.

We watch as a plane descends and snags itself in the net squares like a fly in a spider's web. It too, buzzes frantically in a pitiful, yet ultimately futile protest. The net gives generously at first, as if an errant trampolinist had landed a tad heavily into its bountiful safety. However, the pilot is fighting to save his thousand plus passengers, and agitates too fiercely. The plane rocks this way and that in a tantrum of disbelief. Suddenly the net gives way slightly, and the plane dangles by a wing and a tail, and the net simply snaps back into ruthless geometric order.

Suddenly the pattern of blow-outs takes a ridiculously swift hold, and the familiar network of routain landscape begins to unravel into invisibility before our very eyes. From the far horizon, from all sides, come straight lines shooting across the sky creating a net of electrical rods a mile above our heads. The air rumbles with static. Our clothes and hair arch in resistance. The lines are vaguely red and blue, in varying degrees of transparency and hovering without any apparent means of support.

Then, without warning the plane slips free, falls, and bursts into flames on top of a routain. Another half a mile away another plane drives its stubborn disbelieving nose into the electric mesh. But, what choice do those on the other side of the net have other than to try and pierce it?

Chaos. The routain lights shut off completely all over the townscape. For the first time the heavens look as they might have done when Time begun. Still, twinkling and bright. Below us the world is deathly silent apart from a few rising screams. And the emergency services arrive, clattering and wailing like demented toys. They don't have the facilities to deal with this, but they will play on noisily until they begin to understand. I know that this lock-on gridnet will not shift for a long long time, and if it does it will withdraw as suddenly as it came. One day the rods will simply snatch themselves back into oblivion. I know that this in some form is the end of my world. I know that I will not be leaving this party if the rest of my world does not exist anymore. There, is only here now.

fashion victim

adam wishart

Michelle looked the crest-fallen carnival queen on a rainy day in the suburbs. Tears smudged her mascara. The dress was crumpled and battered. She sat on a cushion by the TV, her face illuminated by 'Drugstore Cowboy'. She snuggled under the blanket, feeling chilled though it wasn't cold.

Really she didn't know why she was so cut up. Like it wasn't that she'd never been stood up before. It wasn't as if some man had never discarded her like puke on the pavement.

She smoked that evening, though she didn't normally.

Earlier she'd gone to the garage to buy Silk Cut to survive the heartbreak. Now her ash-tray was the leftovers of her TV dinner in its plastic tray.

Half watching the movie, she replayed the conversations with this latest disappointment. He'd said he'd call at seven. He'd left the previous morning happy, joking and mincing in his new coat. He'd cared. The sex had been good. Now she tried to persuade herself of all of this, but she felt no passion.

A key turned in the lock. Her flatmate Paul stumbled, pissed, through the doors and slumped on the living room couch. He was rambling. Michelle didn't want to hear another sorry tale of a date without even a goodnight kiss. Either he should stop talking about girls or ask them for a shag.

"Will you shutup Paul," said Michelle. "Can't you see I'm watching the fucking movie."

Paul collapsed into contemplation. He tried to concentrate. But his head was melting. He looked at Michelle and realised she'd been crying.

"You look like a piece of shit Mish."

"You do know how to make a girl feel good."

"You alright? Thought you were taking Sean to dinner."

"He blew me out."

"You're too good for him anyway."

The credits of the film rolled.

"What is it about fucking men, Paul?" asked Michelle. "Why are they such a bunch of unreliable wankers? I don't know why I bother."

Paul couldn't stir a response.

"Except you of course. But you don't count. You're like a woman."

"Thanks," muttered Paul.

"Like three weeks ago, I thought that was it. I'd chuck him. I'd had enough of him. Him not phoning, blowing me out, leching. Then it all seemed to straighten itself out. You know last week he asked me if we were 'going steady'."

"That's cute."

"In the end I don't know why I bother. I wish I fancied women. I bet you they wouldn't be such a hassle."

"Don't bank on it." Paul laughed, then fell asleep on the couch.

Sean was like a squashed chip on a Peckham pavement. His

body sagged in the bath. Baubles of blood ketchupped his arm. The syringe bobbed gently on the ripples.

"Get the fuck up you lazy shit," shouted his sister Noreen. "Get the fuck out of the bath." It was Friday night and she wanted to tart herself up. But for him it was Friday night Out. Sean hadn't turned the tap off. Water trickled down the bathtub and stained the brown carpet black.

"You stupid fucker," shouted Noreen and slammed the front door on her way out. Sean's white skin looked strangely scrubbed. If he hadn't been so well built, he could have been a Sunday morning choirboy, tousled hair and a smile across his battered face. That always made the ladies swoon.

Sean's brother Seamus finished watching 'This Is Your Life'.

He climbed the stairs and banged on the door of the bathroom. "You may have a date, but I need a shit."

His socks went soggy from the wet carpet.

"Sean you alright? You hear me?

"Stop playing fucking games. Sean it's not funny. Look you fucker, you always scare me when you do this. This ain't fucking hide and seek."

Seamus put his ear to the door and listened. "Oi, I'm going to break the fucking door down. You explain that to mum and dad, you big fuck-brain. You tell them you were taking the piss... I'm coming, ready or not."

Seamus took a step back and threw his shoulder against the door. The bolt came away from the old frame and the door swung to.

"Fuck, Sean what the fuck have you done?" His voice trailed. "Sean what have you done?"

Seamus reached over his brother. He slapped him. There was no response. He tried to find Sean's pulse. "Wake up! Stop jesting." Seamus slapped him. Hard across the jaw. Then he slapped him again and again. Nothing happened. Seamus crouched on the floor and held Sean's head in his hands. "You always were a fucking cunt."

Seamus waited until his feet went cold from the damp. He turned the taps off, took the syringe out of Sean's arm and put it in the tobacco box where Sean kept his works. He shook the rest of the smack down the toilet and flushed. He took the box and went downstairs to phone the doctor. As he reached the bottom of the stairs his mother and father came in from the pub.

Seamus took them into the front room and sat them down. "Mum, Sean's dead. He's fucking died."

It was a ritual. Saturday mornings. A hangover, a greasy breakfast and a walk down Portobello Road. Michelle and Paul would barge the Essex sluts and the Japanese tourists dressed like Elvisses. They would browse the market together and come back with pieces of seventies kitsch that neither wanted.

They bumped into Sophie, who was trying to persuade her friends to come out to the country that evening to party in her painted van and make crop circles on the land her family owned. If her family had ever known they'd have revoked her trust fund. For tourists and tabloid journalists would trample the rest of the crop in search of aliens.

Michelle found a fake leopard-skin coat. It only cost a fiver, and it perked her spirits. Paul said that she looked like a million dollars. They walked back to their flat together.

There was no message on the answerphone. She was upset. "He could have phoned," she said. "He could have made an excuse." She got out her address book. "I'm going to phone him. Tell him what a wanker he is."

"If he doesn't phone why should you make the effort? He's not worth it." Paul drawled.

Michelle cuddled herself in her coat. She was resolute. People could not treat her like this anymore. The very least that he owed her was an apology.

She dialled. When Noreen answered, Mish hung up.

"I've started, so I may as well finish."

Michelle dialled again. Noreen answered.

"Is Sean there please?" She was grand in her fur, all ready to say her piece.

Noreen struggled to say the words,

"...Sean's dead."

Michelle's face collapsed like a distressed polaroid. She coiled into a foetal position and wept. Paul crouched by her, feebly stroking her shoulder.

It has been a long hard winter: at the casualty unit where Arsien Kauka works, patients are admitted daily with various kinds of fractures. Mostly old people, on pensions worth less and less each month, out searching for cheap food at street markets. Some of them patiently wait their turn. Others, former bosses and war veterans, try to pull rank by producing ID and pension books. The young orderlies and nurses rudely brush aside

b i r c h s a p

Volha Ipatava

these appeals and claims: "You promised us a brighter future, well—here it is!"

This young rock-and-jeans gang see the future without mysticism: they have studied English, trained in medical school and often take money or gifts from the more knowing patients. Beside them, Arsien, who turned twenty-eight this winter, sometimes feels old and out-of-date: he blushes when the glance of one of the girls lingers on his cheap boots or his tattered, five years old shirt. He'd bought the shirt with his first pay as a doctor, and had just enough over to visit his father and sister bearing new overseas goodies from the city shops. On his return, he'd brought back half a sack of potatoes and a big lump of smoked fat from a pig—reared by his sister under the watchful eye of their aunt, for their tractor driver father was falling apart.

Their father had never come to terms with his wife's death. After the resettlement of "Chernobylites" on the state farm, local lasses had displayed interest in the strong blue-eyed Ivan Khviedar, but none of them measured up to his Antanina. "Not the class," he replied curtly to the urgings of his sister, Arsien's aunt Lizavieta, who between his drinking bouts would dress him up in a new outfit, tow him off to christenings or birth-parties and introduce him to eligible females.

Arsien sympathised with his father and during student vacations he used to take on all the tough work on the holding. Once, when tipsy Ivan made a bet with a local team-leader about who could swim the lake faster and was hauled out semiconscious by some anglers from the city, Arsien showed his mettle and what he'd learned at medical school. From this time on, the villagers turned to him with all their medical troubles, and another time, when the road was washed away in spring and the village cut off from the world, he managed a difficult confinement by talking on the telephone to the local midwife.

Gradually this place which had seemed so strange to the evacuees grew familiar; the dull ache which had settled on them when they left their homes began to fade. All the more so, because the Chernobyl whirlwind which had turned their lives upside down and carried them stunned and confused to the other end of Belarus, gave some of them the chance of an easier life. Arsien got into medical school in the capital without exams, on the basis of his excellent school grades. Over the past ten years he had moved from poverty and semi-orphanhood to working in the capital first at the ambulance station, and then as a paramedic. He acquired a city residence permit by marrying a disabled girl who had a two-roomed flat. She proposed the scheme as a fair exchange for his care and attention, and after being flatmates for several years, they became real friends. Arsien now accepts that in his life there is not only his father and his sister Alena, but also Natallia, whom his aunt and sister keep supplied with potatoes and plain country fare...

After all these years, Arsien still dreams about his mother. Year after year, when the autumn and spring All Souls' Days come round, he thinks of visiting her grave, which might by now be completely overgrown or even washed away by the rains and time.

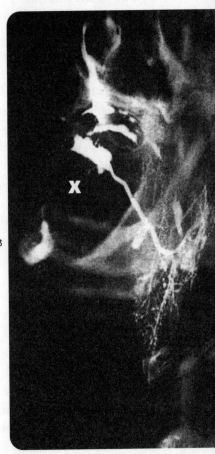

During the first years, evacuees ignored the ban and travelled to the exclusion zone, either to fetch something or to remember their loved ones. But gradually these trips have become more and more dangerous: the howls of feral dogs and emboldened wolves echo all round, roads and paths have become overgrown and washed away, so that the desolation is a barrier in itself.

New life has imperceptibly sunk roots wherever the overwhelming Chernobyl disaster carried it. Arsien's sister now has only faint memories of their mother—at sixteen, she is tired of being mistress of the household and wants to finish school and escape to a life glimpsed in TV soaps, away from the hungry cattle and the drunken ramblings of her father... But Arsien's memories have remained lodged within him; through his student years Mother chased him to lectures after insane nights at the ambulance station filled with cursing and death and blood and all the mysteries of the human body laid bare.

She consoles and instructs him, and her photograph, mounted on white vellum with enormous eyes opened wide to the light and happiness, hangs in his room which is still as poor as a student's. This photograph, glued to the cover torn from an ancient Bible which for three hundred years was handed down in their family from father to son, Arsien managed to stuff inside his jacket during evacuation when they were told to bring only their clothes. His father, overwhelmed by the double grief of the funeral and the evacuation, did not notice and so the photograph remains with the son. And the picture of this girl whose fairytale beauty so radiates happiness helps him remember his mother's face in all its detail—weary now, grown

weak and pale, but still striking in the grey existence of a rural life. He always wanted to help her, to somehow take away the signs of weariness and that other something which he could not name. But all he can do now is not to let her abandoned grave get overgrown...

He departs for the zone as soon as the first snow is off the fields and the roads have dried up. Having spent the night in a local guest-house, he sets out at dawn. The roads to the zone are monitored, but it is possible to go ten kilometres or so before the start of the working day.

Through cracks in the asphalt living, transparent, singing water trickles brightly under the deep blue sky. A light morning wind caresses his face and in the east a bright brick-coloured band grows wider, and the closer he comes to the dark blue arc of the forest, the more it changes, becoming living, pliant and green. Stepping out on this empty road, where as a schoolboy he used to fly down to the Admincentre for medicines for his mother or to interschool contests, it seems to Arsien as if everything is as it had been. Only when he approaches the cemetery, from which the village slopes down into the valley, does he accept that things are not the same.

No birds are singing. Frozen scrub grass cloaks the abandoned houses like wire. Clear and distinct as if carved from crystal, an immense empty space hovers over the entire area. No smoke from the chimneys, no movement of human or animal, no trace of a child. There is an evil and encompassing peace. The black, waterlogged fields, the white patches of snow in the gullies, the sandy road damp from the night, all this seems unreal, like a dream, when you want to shout and run, but you cannot move... For a long time, Arsien stands on the hilltop. Then he descends into the valley, to his own home with its long broken lock and smashed windows, and the blackened, tattered cloth draping the house shrine, and the skeleton of some animal by the threshold. Later, leaving for the cemetery rucksack on shoulder and trowel in hand, it comes into his head: perhaps it was the dog, Sharyk, who had wandered around uncared for after they left and had returned home to die?

Arsien finds the hard, compacted mound with its leaning cross immediately, as if someone is leading him by the hand. And the whole time that, bent double, he tends the grave with its thin metal label imprinted with the letters of his mother's name, the feeling of some presence never leaves him. On the level, yellow surface of the grave he spreads a cloth embroidered by his sister and sets out on it bread, onion, smoked pork fat and some red eggs that have been blessed in church. It is then that the man appears, from behind an old oak on the edge of the cemetery.

Older than Arsien, in a tattered greasy tunic and a cap with earflaps, he does

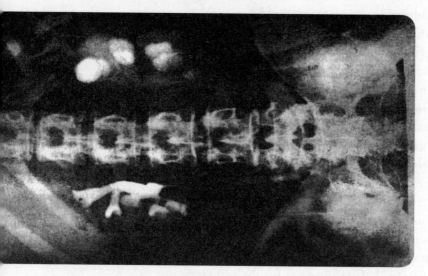

not appear to be local; swarthy and hooknosed, he has a cautious, timid gait like a lynx. He holds a jug in both hands. Arsien, who is feverishly groping in his rucksack for his knife, relaxes, for the stranger makes an attempt to smile, and speaks in Russian, the words fractured with a Caucasian accent:

"Local, da? Who you come remember? Momma, da?"

Arsien nods briefly. The stranger places

the jug on the bench beside the adjacent grave, in which Arsien's grandma is buried, and asks warily:

"Cigarette you got?"

Arsien takes out an opened packet. The Caucasian lights up and inhales, his hands trembling slightly.

"And vodka you got, da? I got juice, your local stuff. We drink, da?"

Arsien cautiously takes out the bottle. What are you to do, that's the way of things. Memorial rites without spirits just aren't memorial rites. Mother never used to drink, but he has brought a shot-glass, to be filled and left on the grave. Taking out both glasses, he says shortly:

"You'll drink from mine."

"But I got glass," the man takes a small enamelled metal cup from a pocket, and extends his other hand: "I Mutalib. I from Chechenia. You know Chechenia? War, da? But me... I want live... I want to West, da?"

Arsien hardly feels the spirits go down. But when he chases it with birch sap, his heart burns. He remembers the black day when they evacuated the village. The lamenting of women, the howling of children, the dust covered buses. He and his father and sister, stunned with something even more terrible; Mother had died in the very night before the evacuation, as if wanting to stay here forever, among her forebears. There was no time for a proper wake, Auntie just handed out spirits and sausage to everyone on the bus, and he, a tenth-grader, drank and drank birch sap straight from the bottle, his teeth chattering feverishly against the glass...

Arsien has never drunk birch sap since that day. But Mutalib's gift takes him by surprise and the cool piercingly familiar drink seems to tear something inside him: he weeps, and tells the wanderer about his family and the evacuation, about how his mother used to sing and dance and undo the evil eye and hiw she knew every herb in the meadows. The stranger interrupts to tell of his attempt to flee to Germany by paying a "guide" five thousand American dollars—almost all he'd brought with him when he fled the war. How the "guide" abandoned him, and

23

the customs men who caught him took the rest, gutted him and left him on the Polish-Belarusian frontier. For three months now he has been living in this terrible peopleless, deserted, strange village, not even daring to go to the Admincentre store...

Afterwards, as suddenly as if hit by lightning or a stroke, Arsien falls asleep, his back resting against a young birch. When he opens his eyes, the Caucasian is gone and Mother's shot-glass stands empty on the grave before him.

There is no one around. The earth, slightly warmed now, gives out a strong fragrance. Needles of young grass pierce the soil here and there. Dry leaves whisper in the light breeze, and from close by comes the ringing sound of drops falling. Arsien gets up heavily; he looks for the jug, but it is upside down, empty and dry. He picks it up and walks over to a slender birch with gleaming bark at the edge of the cemetery. Yes, the Caucasian collected his birch sap here. Maybe the birches in the valley have no sap left, or maybe he simply prefers it here

at the top...

The murky, flashing droplets run swiftly down the bark, chiming on a root sticking up out of the earth, and breaking up into little splashes. The jug is quickly half full, and Arsien once again drinks and drinks the birch sap, not wanting to remember that everything grown in this earth holds danger, like poisoned apples in the fairytale his Mother used to tell... And the drops go on falling and breaking up in splashes on his boots.

"It should be bound up. The birch will die." The thought flashes into his mind, but he turns away to collect his rucksack. Nothing in this place makes any sense.

He has left the cemetery, when he suddenly turns back, and hurries to the birch tree. Taking out some sticking plaster, he carefully places it over the gashes. Let it go on living here, let it rustle under the boundless sky.

Now he can return to the city.

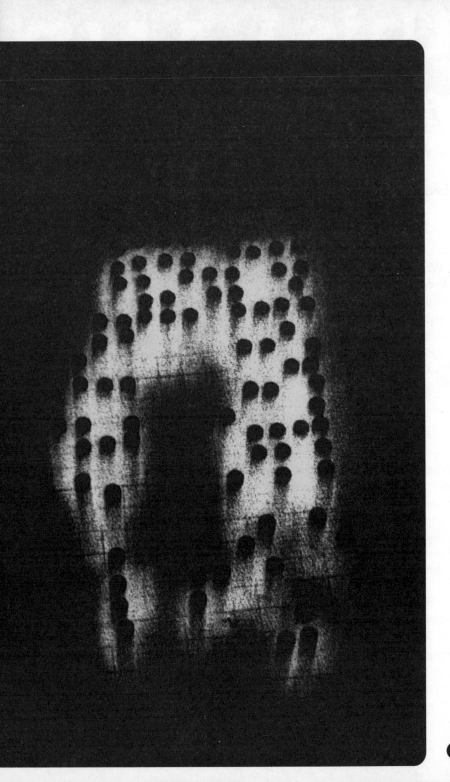

this LAND is our LAND

Laura Pachkowski

"So," he asks waving his scissors, "Where do you come fr... ?" Abdul pauses as he notices the bald spots dotting my scalp. He inspects as if for nits and then composes himself quickly. He says again, "Where *are* you from?" and lowers my lanky blonde strands.

Newtown was a boom town toy-town propped beneath the orange midnight sun and above a black tar pit. A northern town, but not far enough north to be of interest and not far enough south to lie on a line of permanent migration. Even flocks of Canada geese bypassed Newtown with contempt.

On the edge of this temporary town, to the south, an oil refinery pumped 200-tons-of-crude-oil-a-day into pipelines and pumped 200-tons-of-sulphur-waste-a-day into the Athabasca River flowing North. There was only one road into Newtown

which was also the only road out. In the sub-Arctic dead of winter, this lifeline was closed and supplies were flown in.

People only came to Newtown to work in the oil refinery. And then they got the hell out. My father came to Newtown to work but he was in no great hurry to get out. A specialist extraction engineer, he operated the giant toothed Bucket Wheel that extracted petroleum from the tar pit. He had his own personal dialogue with the North; he respected it *to a point*, and then he fed on it, to feed us. For him, there was no symbiosis, only survival.

Newtown is dead now; a ghost town. The buildings remain but the people are gone. Now that I live in the city, now that I am losing my hair, memories of Newtown dance like wayward atoms on the fringes of my mind. I am an artist. I paint abstract

blobs. I work from memory.
Black. Tar black. Oil black,
sometimes with orange bubbles.

We lived at first in an
aluminium unit in a trailer park.
Our neighbours were mixed blood
Metis who had worked hard to get
out of the ditches of the
reservation. I met
Mabel, a two
hundred pound
Metis who
carried a
shotgun and I
let her cut off my
long blonde hair with a flick
knife. I guess it was a bad
haircut because Dad worked
harder and moved us into a
bungalow in the new sub-division
of Thickwood Heights. I was seven.
Mom was in the hospital reading
magazines and my new brother
lay in a glass box. I was in the
bungalow with Dad. He lay on the
sofa watching the news. My Star
Wars bubble gum cards were
scattered on the shag carpet.

‹...armaments... missiles...›

"Dad?"

‹...neutron particles with no
electric charge...›

"Dad?"

‹...kills by intense radiation...
little damage to buildings...›

"What!"

"Are the Russians going to
bomb us?" A wasp smacked into
the living room window. Don't
bother them and they won't
bother you, as Mom liked to say.

"Hell no! we're safe from
the Ruskies up here," he said
picking at a scab in his ear.

"But what about the plant —
we have oil, won't they bomb our
oil?"

"We'll get in the car and
drive to the farm... "

My Dad's contingency, forty
acres of land,
was a twenty-
five hour
drive to the
southeast of
Newtown. His
farm lay next to my
grandparents farm. Their parents
had been Russian immigrants,
though my Dad called them
Lubovian Carpathian Ukrainians.
My friends at school were all of
French or Irish extraction, except
for Mabel's son, Mickey C, who
was Metis. He swore a lot and
Miss Scutts often washed his
mouth out with soap. She said he
was dirty.

"But Dad, what if they bomb
us while we're driving there?"

My Dad snorted and changed the channel. I didn't like the idea that my ancestors could kill me. We had little experience of death or murder in Newtown, only of industrial accidents.

Soon after that, Dad bought me a television. I watched it alone in my room.

On the CTV National News, Lloyd Newman announced that a Russian Arms Plan had been revealed.

‹...major population areas; Montreal, Toronto, Vancouver and a few select targets in the North; The Cold Lake Air Force Base, Yellowknife, Tuktoyuktuk and NEWTOWN...›

That night I slept badly. I dreamt of detonation. A sonic boom so loud my eardrums perforated. Of melting faces. I woke up to orange light blasting into my bedroom. THE BIG ONE! THIS IS IT! I got up, stumbled on my pyjama bottoms and ran to my window. In the same empty, suburban streets the electricity board had only changed the bulbs from white to orange. THIS IS ONLY A TEST. Newtown slept.

I forgot about nuclear bombs and started to worry about fire. Being trapped. Being burned alive. One afternoon, poking at the dead fish washed up on the banks of the Athabasca, I saw smoke billowing above the trees. I knew from the Yogi Bear campaign (Hey, Hey Boo-boo Beware), it was forest fire season. The fire attached to this smoke was close to annihilating Newtown. First, it attacked a poorer sub-division on the north side of town. Families were evacuated and rounded up in yellow school buses. They watched their cheap, bought-and-paid-for homes burn to the ground. Newtown raged.

I panicked and packed my comics in brown paper bags and put them in my closet. I sat with them and waited.

Dad poked his head in my closet and said, "What the HELL are you doing Anna?"

"Waiting."

"Waiting for what?"

"For the fires—in case we have to evacuate..."

"GET OUT OF THAT CLOSET AND GO HELP YOUR MOTHER COOK SUPPER."

I still dream about fires. Burning alive. Of being blasted into nothingness. Of being sucked into black quick sand. My latest exhibition opens at a gallery in Soho. It's called Tar Baby. I'm sponsored by a Canadian whiskey distillery.

Dad returned to the sofa. A torrential downpour doused the fires a few days later. I returned to the river where yellow foam washed ashore, smelling of rotten eggs or of Dad's feet. In the foam, more dead fish. Newtown heaved.

I forgot about fires and started to worry about smells.

My best friend, Jasmine, lived next door. Her family were Sikhs but they came from Kenya. Her Dad was my Dad's boss at work and they had a bigger house than us. I though they were exotic. There was a zebra skin hanging on their living room wall. They ate pastel poppadoms (sent from India) with Kentucky Fried Chicken take-aways. Jasmine's mother didn't go out much and kept fit by pedalling a stationary exercise bike. Her sister had long, jet black hair and a nose ring. Her Dad had long, jet black hair and wore a white turban to cover it up. He also wore a ceremonial knife. The neighbours hoo-ha'd. Dad called him a terrorist. I thought he was glamourous.

One afternoon, Dad said I couldn't play with Jasmine anymore. He sent me to my room. I heard him bellow;

"...not playin' with Pakis... their damn smell wafts into our back yard."

My father opened my door without knocking and shouted "GO HELP YOUR MOTHER COOK SUPPER." She'd cooked Chicken Kiev, sauerkraut and kulbasa. I said to Mom, "I can't eat this, it smells!" An American F-15 fighter jet flew over our house. Newtown ducked.

There was an oil crisis. The price of a barrel went up and Dad cheered up. He bought another car. He left the engine running while he ambled into the local liquor store. He grinned nasty grins when the television showed pictures of people in California queuing around the block to buy gas. He started to polish his rifles. He talked about war.

The Cold War, the threat of nuclear annihilation didn't end as much as fizzle out. Nine years later, and never out of Newtown, when I was sixteen, there was a school field trip to the Mediterranean. Events in Libya convinced my Dad that the world was unsafe. I couldn't go, he said. He told me to get a job instead. There weren't any, so I spent the summer skateboarding along the sidewalks of Newtown, above the bubbling tar pit and beneath the scorching summer sun. I had a green mohican that would have done Mabel, my childhood hairdresser, proud. My ripped t-shirt had the slogan:

MUTATE NOW.
WHY WAIT FOR THE POST-BOMB RUSH?

There was a lot of corked aggression in Newtown that summer. The neighbour's kids threw stones. Men in pick-up trucks threw empty beer bottles at me. Dad taught my brother how to drive. He was only nine. I had long forgotten about bombs

and fires and smells. I started to worry about men...

I saw Mabel once more before I left Newtown. She was lying in a ditch, swilling from a bottle of Canadian Club. A royal shade of purple had formed around her left eye. I don't think she recognised me when she mumbled, "da land is da only thing that lafsts... da land." Newtown swallowed her up.

Dad did leave eventually. He had to. When the oil refinery had throttled the life out of the land, everyone left. Some people even took their cheap, bought-and-paid-for homes with them on eighteen-wheel trucks. Only the native Indians were left. The town folded like a story book. My Dad moved to his farm in the South. My mother didn't. The land remains.

"Where are you from?" Abdul's whine jerks me back. He's snipping at my roots. I don't mention these mutinous memories. I say nothing but I am convinced that I am from the land and only the land lasts.

He rolls his eyes. Another clump of my hair falls to the floor and I'm wondering if I should dye what's left of it black.

THE ROOFTOPS

by Amy Prior

What you put into your body, you get out. That's what Angel told me on the roof. Angel abhors animal foods of all kinds and thinks the cruelty of killing destroys your karma. She grows all her own vegetables in her own allotment and fertilises them using horse manure. They taste nice but you have to remember to wash them first.

She met my flatmate Ricki at a party three months ago in a mansion block on Shoot Up Hill. They got drunk on ginger wine and left together early to look at the stars. I've seen her once since then. Ricki took me along to see her on stage. She plays bass guitar in a band at the weekends and this, I suppose, is how everything started. I like to take photos, and she wanted publicity shots for two big agent guys in the music industry. She had heard from Ricki, who heard from Stasz, who been told by Yola, that Jimmy and Johnny were going to be there at the big gig, and she wanted to be prepared.

So that Thursday I found myself in Soho at the bakery where she worked. She didn't have long, only her lunch hour. I wasn't very confident of being able to do her justice in such a short space of time.

"Don't worry child, I've got the key to the roof," she said. "We'll go up there and you'll take some good shots. All that space up there. All that air. Now wait a minute while I go and put some lippy on."

I waited a while. She'd given me an organic pain aux raisins. Still soft and vanillery, even though it had been baked more than three hours ago.

"She's taking you up top?" said the woman working with Angel.

"Yes, I think so."

"You mind your step up there," she said. "One slip and you'll be no more."

She took a bite from an eclair and smiled. Cream lined the corners of her mouth and perspiration ran in rivulets down her chin and neck, forming a dark stream down the front of her blouse. "We'll be careful, Bertha," Angel said, smiling brightly.

She led me to a door that opened outside and we climbed up a black metal winding stairway. 250 steps, easily.

"Don't look down," said Angel. She'd done this before, I could tell. She ran up, every now and then checking to see how I was doing with all my camera equipment. I'll say now, I took too much gear. I didn't know what she had planned, so I'd got my indoor stuff as well. I wasn't leaving it downstairs to bake with Bertha.

Up on the roof the air was chill. I was glad of my muff. It had rained the night before and there were a few kidney-shaped puddles on the uneven asphalt.

"What do I do?" said Angel.

She began fussing with her hair, running her fingers through the front to ruffle it up a bit. It was one of those short styles that are so fashionable at the moment. Kind of feathery at the sides and bleached white so she looked like a kind of holy street urchin. Kind of seventies; kind of nineties; kind of unreal against her cocoa-coloured skin.

"You know," she said, as she was moving about to find a space to sit down. "You can walk on these roofs all the way to Charing Cross."

"Really?" I said, taking the opportunity to capture her animated expression. It was always good to get them talking. Smile, be interested, and they'll start to relax.

"If you start here you can walk along Brewer Street, over the post office and then it's a straight line down to the river. Can you see the river over there?"

"Yes," I said.

Her face wasn't focussing. I moved the zoom in and out but it still looked blurry.

"What are you doing? I haven't got all day, girl," she said.

I had to start taking control. I wasn't used to this. I'm no professional, but I wasn't going to let on. Photography's just a hobby. Something I do at weekends. I'll go to the park or the woods or up west or to my niece's christening and take snaps and then develop them in the darkroom at the community centre. Angel thinks I'm big time. Ricki gave her the wrong impression and now I think she's realising.

"We need some action shots," I said. I thought: at least they are meant to be blurred. So she strode over to the vent which expelled the hot air from the bakery ovens.

"Shame I'm not in a skirt. I could be like Marilyn Monroe," she said, raising her voice at the end of the sentence making it a question the American way. She crouched down low over the grating and tossed her hair over the air flow. I could almost see the prints. A shock of white lightning on a milky brown circle with red cupid lips and eyes. I forgot to say about the eyes. Well, they were the greenest green I've ever seen. Like tiny round apples hanging from her face. And the strangest thing was the way they almost glowed. I'd seen them before in the darkness of the Fire Club and they were almost fluorescing then.

"That's great," I said.

"Let's take five," she said. "I've got to eat."

She broke open a pitta and began spreading hummus over it.

"What are you having?"

"I've got some Polos," I said. "I'll have something at home. "

"You know," she said, "you've really got to watch what you eat. Bertha downstairs, she eats three cream cakes every day and she's the most unhappy person I know. What you put in your body is what you get you out. Remember that. You don't look too well yourself. Late night last night?

"Not really." I thought of last night. Sausage and chips and EastEnders and Brookside videoed from the night before and then on the phone to my mum. "No, fairly quiet actually."

"Well you ought to look after yourself more. You ought to eat more of this."

"What's that?"

"Alfafa. Full of B vitamins. You know the best tonic?" she said, beginning to smile.

"What's that?"

"Urine. Drink a glass of it from your first pee of the day. You'll soon feel great. There's lots of nutrients in it."

"Really?"

"Uh-huh. Oh god. It's past two and I've got to go down. Have you got enough shots?"

"I'm sure that'll be fine."

"I'll come and see the prints at the weekend." And when I turned round she had gone. I didn't even hear her feet on the stairs.

She really got me thinking. That night I took a long look at myself in the mirror in the bathroom. "Jane," I said to my reflection. "Jane. look at those shadows under your eyes. Look at that red patch of skin round your lips. Notice the suppurating sore under your nose. You've got to heed Angel's advice. Look after yourself. What you put in your body, you get out."

So the next day I started on a new regime. I ate Bran Buds for breakfast. I ate wholemeal sandwiches and fruit for lunch and hummus and pitta for tea. I did this for three days. My sore cleared up. My shadow faded. I was doing well, I thought, but there was something missing.

I woke at seven the next morning and, as usual, headed downstairs for the toilet. I tried to open the door, but there was something in the way. I fumbled around in the dark. Ricki had left a bucket there. He had been cleaning the windows the day before. I took the bucket into the toilet and squatted down. Let's just try it, I thought. Then I took the bucket into the kitchen and decided which glass to use. A tumbler was too much. I chose a wine glass and poured myself a glass of the warm, full-bodied liquid. At first it tasted of water, but then there was a strong salty taste, like warm sea. I started by gulping it, but then it went down smoothly: a warm drink you don't have to make in a kettle! Soon I became accustomed to this routine and every day for the next three I drank this warm sea. The red patch of skin on my lips healed after a few days.

On Friday night, Ricki and some of his friends came round. Usually on occasions like these I make myself scarce. But this time it was different. Angel had brought some organic cakes she had made at the bakery specially for tonight. She offered me one.

"You'll love these cakes, Jane," she said, smiling up at me. "They're spicy, full of nutmeg and coconut and lots of other things," she said, looking around the room and sharing glances with the others. "Well, ok, just one. You know I'm on my diet."

"Oh no, these are good cakes," said Angel. "They are good for you. You can eat as many as you like and you'll feel good."

So I ate a few and she was right. We played cards. All the time Ricki smoked his rolled up cigarettes and shared them with the other people in the room. People I didn't know.

"You know Jane, you've not been yourself this week, have you?" Ricki said.

"Meaning what?" I asked.

"You've been different. Happy. You've got more energy. You went to see a film last night. You haven't been out for months."

"Yes, it's true." I said. I looked at him and the most curious thing happened. His face shrunk to half its size. His beard, his pallor and his long curls, compressed. It was like I was seeing a stranger. I looked away.

"That's good," said Angel.

I looked at her. There was something different about her as well. A glow above her head. In a sort of circle. And her T-shirt, emblazoned with the words Raving Rock Chick, developed white and feathery attachments at the sides.

"I think I have to go to bed now," I said quietly.

"Don't you want another cake?" asked Angel, as I left the room.

The next morning I felt fine. Then I drank my glass of warm sea. Soon after, last night's feelings returned. Still, I carried on regardless. That's the spirit gal, my old mother would say. I caught the tube to Oxford Street and started on my shopping: a birthday present for mum and a set of napkins from John Lewis. But then something very strange happened. All the shoppers lost their faces. I was surrounded by crowds of faceless bodies. I had to go to lie down somewhere quiet where there were no people. I walked and walked but I did not know where I was or where I was going. But then I found myself in a familiar street. A newsagents and then a bakers. A large faceless woman was standing behind a shop window. Bertha! Big Bertha!

I went through the door of the bakers. "She's not here," Bertha said. "It's her day off."

"It's not her I've come to see," I said. "It's the roof."

"Oh yes? " she said.

Realising this may have sounded strange, I said: "Yes, I need to take some background shots...for the photos."

"I see," she said, not seeing at all. How could she?

"Well, you better go up."

And she waved her ample arm towards the door.

Out on the roof things were less complicated. There were no faceless people to contemplate, only the beep-beep of car horns far away and the hissing of hot air forcing its way through the air vent.

Then I heard her voice: "You know, you can walk on these roofs all the way to Charing Cross. You walk along to Brewer Street, over the post office and it's a straight line down to the river."

I rose from my lying position and began to walk. I edged over the crack onto the next building. It was difficult negotiating the fire escape, but I didn't have my courts on, so I managed it. When I came to the post office I sat down for a while on a concrete block and considered the rest of the journey. The river was quite close now. There was a cloud of mist just above it. It was still quite early and the city had not yet warmed up.

As I stared, the mist seemed to be getting bigger and moving my way. Past the bridge, past Leicester Square, past the big department stores along Oxford Street. It began to glow orange and then yellow and then the brightest white, and from it descended a figure with a glow above its head and white and feathery attachments at the sides. The blood rushed from my head to all my internal organs. Fight or flight, I thought. That's the way adrenalin works.

"Jane, Jane," she said (for it was a sweet and gentle female voice). "You've learnt that what you put in your body, you get out. You ate some good cakes last night that made you and your body see the truth. Now come with me and learn some more. She extended her hand down to me.

For a moment I felt a sharp pain at my sides. I looked and saw some feathery wings that matched hers. Then for a moment—it could only have been a moment—I moved up, up and away into the hands of the gods.

ALIENS

EMMA KATE MARTIN

It was the television Cassie had dreamed about. Its screen was as flat as a pond on a windless day, and apparently as deep. Cassie could sit for seconds on end gazing into it even when it was switched off: as black as a pond on a windless night, as flawless as a pond and as seamless as the sky. The night Cassie brought Grace back to her flat she took her straight to the television, not to bed. Instead of sex they watched late night music videos and ads for Pepsi and Calvin Klein. In the flickering blue light Grace looked less real than the faces on the screen: by morning her face was already familiar and Cassie was bored. She was used to switching channels whenever the pace slowed.

Grace moved in only a week or so later. In the months that followed Cassie would look back in despair and try to remember exactly why it was she had opened her door to Grace, cut her a key, given her equal rights over her home and especially over her television—the sight of the remote control in Grace's hand caused her heart to race with fury—but it was all a blank. She could remember nothing, except that the hire purchase payments had been hard to keep up with and Grace would pay half the rent.

For a while Cassie had kind of enjoyed the company, if that's what it was. Grace washed the dishes every few days. She brought home bottles of imported lager stolen from the bar where she worked. She swelled Cassie's wardrobe with glorious clothes which fitted Cassie perfectly, of course, both of them being exactly the same size.

Then little things started to bother Cassie. Evidence started to mount up and soon it was unmistakeable: Grace wasn't the person she had thought at all. Cassie had assumed, because they wore the same labels and had similar designs scratched with ink into their skin, that they were compatible, even identical. Waking up to Grace in the morning was like waking up to her own reflection; used to only considering surfaces, Cassie was horrified to realise that there might be something going on inside Grace's pretty, shaved head, and that thing might not be what was going on inside her own. She started to want to talk to Grace. She started to want Grace to talk back. What are you thinking? she'd say, and Grace would say: Nothing. Cassie suspected her of lying. She wanted to know the truth.

In frustration Cassie tried to pick fights with Grace; but Grace wouldn't be picked with. As if she didn't care enough to win an argument, she'd answer Cassie's carefully gathered evidence with: Whatever you say. It was like pushing against air. Cassie fantasised about throwing Grace to the kitchen floor and pounding her head against the linoleum: at least then she'd have to fight back. Grace, despite her frail build and skinny wrists, was quick and strong. Arm-wrestling Cassie in a pub one night she held her ground effortlessly. They were evenly matched. A kind of intimacy, Cassie supposed: but then Grace had looked her in the eye and slackened her grip. For Cassie, these victories were hollower than any defeat. Grace already half-way to the bar to buy the next round; Cassie's arm tingling from the pressure of the table against her elbow; onlookers smiling softly and sipping their vodkas—as a snapshot it could hardly be more beautiful. But like a snapshot, its underside was white and shiny. Cassie, whose lungs it turned out were healthy and pink and definitely in 3-D, found herself gasping for air. Meanwhile Grace, if she had come across a man dying of thirst in the middle of a desert, might have offered him an advertisement for bottled soda, torn from a magazine.

When aliens landed on the mid-western prairies, Grace betrayed no flicker of interest.

It's funny, babbled Cassie, how aliens always land in America, how they always fly in on cigar-shaped shuttles, and look pretty much like we expect them to. Don't you think it's odd how we guess they'll be small and green with glazed yellow eyes, and then they are, they really are. Grace blinked carefully, twice, and did not answer. The flying saucer was spotted by over a hundred people; either a whole town was in collusion or aliens really did land. At the point of impact there was only a smoking crater and some suspicious looking footprints where fresh drifts of snow hadn't reached. What do you think happened? asked Cassie, ready with an explanation that would make sense from both a sociological and a geological point of view. Grace said: I don't care. She picked up the remote and flicked through the channels. Cassie could've pointed her own lean and crooked finger towards a friendlier planet. Do you want a beer? she said. No, said Grace.

It was Cassie of course, of course it was Cassie.

She was the one who'd changed. Suddenly prying, trying to mount her own invasion, talking faster and faster when previously she had been silent. If Cassie had only been content like Grace, content with what was visibly fine, instead of burrowing and scratching. But Cassie had fallen victim to the instinct to dissect. And like the CIA with their tiny frozen corpses cut ever so neatly, arranged in cross-sections under microscope slides, categorised, alphabeticised, Cassie found herself in no position to empathise. Post-mortems on aliens reveal less than you'd expect. Dead bodies are mute on so many subjects. If Cassie had cracked open Grace's head with a rock, no secrets would've leaked out, only blood. Sometimes she wanted to do it anyway.

That Grace had secrets Cassie had no doubt. There was the matter of the scars, for one thing, which criss-crossed lattice-like across the backs of both shoulders, near no major artery: too random and too deep for decoration, yet even enough— surely—to suggest the infliction had been purposeful. Cassie longed to trace those trails along Grace's skin with her finger-tips but did not dare: though she imagined wandering through Grace's world, charting it like a foreign planet, as hot as Mars, or cold as Venus.

Aliens crept fearfully from the ruins of their craft. This time of year the prairies were snow-covered, and looked to last forever whichever way you went. Aliens, not being sociable by nature and concussed into the bargain, set off in different directions, radiating out from their point of landing. Every step of their little green legs carried them further from each other; beyond shouting or burbling distance; and the snow was starting to fall again. Aliens were cold. Lost on the prairies, a long, long way from home. Humans huddle together for warmth; aliens find the proximity of other cold bodies only causes their own temperature to drop.

These things were acceptable: standing side by side with bottled beer in their hands, leaning against the bar and kissing hello and then good-bye to the prettier boys; hanging out in clubs where the music was loud and talking was not worth the effort; having girl-girl sex. So picture this: Cassie's flat, which is on the twentieth floor of a council block and which has no curtains because no-one within a mile is high enough to see in; the sky as seamless as a television screen; the lights of the city below; and Cassie, who of course is beautiful, and strong though she is small, failing again and again and again and again to get what it is she wants. Grace's armour never cracks. If you could see them asleep together you would long to live the way they do.

Of course for Cassie, like for everyone else, no fascination can burn forever. Either it consumes you completely and leads you to momentous acts of violence or love—Cassie shooting Grace between the eyes, or throwing herself in front of a bullet to save her—or the fascination dies. For Cassie, who wasn't used to waiting for things she couldn't get in the first flush of desire, there was a point when she realised she was no longer interested in what Grace thought. Just like that. As if a switch had clicked, though turning on or off exactly what inside her, it was hard to say. They would sit in front of the television just like on that very first night and in the symmetry of their bodies and in the silhouettes of their faces there was nothing to indicate that anything had changed.

Things returned to normal. Cassie worked her shifts and Grace worked hers. Aliens sneaked across the snowy fields, startled by and startling small birds whose eyes were black and shiny, whose wings were stiff with the cold. Darkness flooded the flat landscape. From the top of their block Cassie and Grace could see for miles, and as winter closed in they took to watching thrillers and action movies with

plenty of explosions while the rain beat against the windows
and the gas fire hissed. Aliens reached the continent of
Europe. Aliens crawled through the channel tunnel and
staggered onto English soil. A new beat was playing in the
city's clubs: Cassie and Grace danced like they were born
to it, and in the way they moved and with the dimness
of the lights it was almost impossible to tell them
apart: everyone said so: people even asked if they
were sisters, to which Grace would not answer
and Cassie would only shake her head no. It
didn't take long, all things considered. Aliens
arrive in the neighbourhood. Aliens make for
your bed. They lodge themselves between
your sheet and your duvet and suck away at
the warmth but give nothing in return. You
can't blame them. It's just how they are.
What Cassie learnt was that you can't
beat them, but you can't join them either.
They just arrive one day and before you
know it you've been colonised.

It's the TV that attracts
them. Like the seamless
black sky on a cloudy night,
it reminds them of home.

MICHAEL RIVER
LIKE MAYBE

The car ground out a shrapnel of brown drizzle from the wet road. Ben slouched in the back seat watching the night and rain. He breathed patches of fog on the glass and drew simple faces in them. He said, "You know I've never, I mean with a woman."

"Not me, stupid," snapped the driver. "I'm just the agent."

"Oh." He looked away from her rearview eyes.

The car wove a fast hypnotic route down the city's dark blocks, closing in through a sleazy riverside district to pull up outside the grand ramshackle facade of the Sideshow Hotel, teetering on the water's edge.

The agent lead Ben into the foyer. A half-blown chandelier cast musty light over a group of boys already waiting, loitering on faded floral couches, fidgeting or dozing. The agent counted them and checked her watch. "Enough, let's hope. OK, time to get started." She herded the boys to the lift. "Third floor," she told them when the doors opened. She sent them up in two groups, crammed into the tiny box, then followed by herself. The lift opened on a corridor muffled in velvety drapes and wallpaper.

"You first," the agent told one of them. "Through that door, down to the end. He'll tell you what to do."

One by one the boys went through the door. They never stayed more than ten minutes, and as each came out the agent uttered a small despondent sigh, handed over a tenner and sent him on his way.

A man in a black suit arrived with two more boys in tow. He looked the waiting line over and sneered.

"What's this? Chapter 15?"

"16," said the agent, not looking up.

The man in the black suit took a seat beside her and shook his head. "I really don't know why you put up with it."

"Yes you do," she said. "15%. Genius can have its quirks."

A sulky boy slouched out after barely five minutes beyond the door. "Creep," he muttered over his shoulder.

"Next," announced the agent.

Ben pushed the door open and entered the suite. A short hallway led past several closed doors to a large dim room. The curtains were drawn but the windows open. Propped against the lefthand wall was a collection of age-speckled mirrors in ornate gilt frames.

The fat man sat by a standard lamp in one corner. When he stood his face was half-hidden in the lampshade's penumbra. "Do you know who I am?"

Ben shrugged. "She said you're a writer."

"But you don't read."

Against the righthand wall was an old fashioned writing desk. Beside it a chaise longue rested on gilt balled claws. The curtain parted briefly to allow a glimpse of the black river. He said, "Well, it is a bit old fashioned, isn't it? I mean, like ballet or something."

The fat man smirked. "Could not agree with you more. Take your clothes off."

Ben pulled his shirt over his head. His various reflections arrayed along the wall stretched in unison, dusty limbs lifting, falling. He took off his shoes, his trousers, his underwear. The room was chilly and his skin instantly goose-pimpled.

"Mm," said the fat man. "Turn around please."

Ben turned slowly. When he faced around again the fat man was undoing his belt. "No red, no brown," he warned. "I told the lady."

"Shh." The fat man dropped his pants. "You'll find I'm not too demanding. Let me show you something you won't have seen before."

The writer's belly cast a big shadow. Ben had heard that fat men had small ones, but even so he couldn't make out anything between his legs. He came close and dropped to a crouch. Where the fat man's prick should have been was only a ridge of pink flesh, a scar in a crooked S-shape.

"Jesus," said Ben.

"You can touch it if you like."

Reluctantly Ben put his finger on the scar. It felt like the plastic seam on a doll. "How did it happen?"

"The rage of a jealous lover. Or was it a dog, that afterward escaped and roams the city still, with a craving for that particular meat? I forget. Maybe it was only a car-crash. Maybe I was a novelty weightlifter who overextended himself. So to speak."

"Which was it?"

"Take your pick." He shrugged. "You know they say people who have lost an arm or a leg are supposed to be able to still feel it? You heard of that?"

"Yeah, sure."

"See, sometimes I get that feeling." His pudgy fingers traced out an imaginary shape. "If I close my eyes I feel like maybe..."

"What do you want me to do?" asked Ben.

"I want you to suck me."

Ben looked up at him. The fat man's eyes were already closed.

He bent forward and parted his lips, imagining the bulb tip of a fat prick and the taste of it on his tongue. He slid his lips over, teasing gently with his teeth. He licked his tongue around it and took it deep into his throat.

The fat man's hand dropped onto his head and started rocking him. They both moved like that in silence except for their hoarse breathing that slowly got faster.

The fat man quivered and subsided. "Enough," he said weakly and pushed Ben's head away.

Ben got to his feet. He probed his tongue round his mouth, as if looking for ectoplasmic cum. The fat man pulled up his trousers. He buttoned them one-handed and gestured to the couch. "Lie down over there, please. Face up."

Ben lay on the couch. A river wind riffled the curtains and stirred loose papers on the desk. Taking a pen from the cluttered desktop the fat man stood over him. The sound of distant traffic.

"My little muse," the fat man said and smiled. "Now." He raised his pen. "Hold still."

He carefully inscribed the number 16 on Ben's clavicle, and started writing underneath.

The pen crawled across Ben's skin like a small insect, and at first he could barely stop himself swatting it away. But after a while he almost enjoyed its specific caress. Eventually he dozed off under the gentle pressure of the nib.

He had barely started a dream about seagulls and lightbulbs when the fat man woke him: "Turn over please." Ben glanced down. His body was covered to the knee in elegant cursive, ink that glistened like the river. He rolled onto his front, resting his chin on his crossed arms. The pen swooped at once to prick his shoulder.

He could not get back to sleep. He studied what he could see of the room: the wallpaper, cream parchment flocked with unpleasant crimson patterns; the toothed coving spotted with decay; the ceiling of faintly flaking plaster; crash-and-burn blowfly carcasses in the lamp.

He closed his eyes again and followed the progress of the pen, across his back, wriggling around each of his vertebrae, down to his side, then over to start again on the other flank. He tried to decipher what was being written. Occasionally he thought he could make out single words, mainly parts of speech like "a" or "the" or "like", but once or twice he imagined he had the gist of entire sentences:

YOUR
HANDS
WERE
COLD

and:

I WISH
YOU'D
NEVER
TOUCHED
ME.

The fat man worked his way slowly down to the small of Ben's back, to his buttocks and the backs of his thighs. He wrote down one leg and then the other. Just above the back of Ben's right knee he finished with a jabbed full stop.

"Ouch!"

The fat man tossed his pen aside. "That's all. You can go."

Ben grabbed his clothes from the floor.

"Careful," said the fat man, flopping into an armchair. He poured himself a whisky. "My agent will be *most* displeased should you smudge the ink." He pointed out a threadbare bathrobe. "Wear that."

"Mr Cowper." Ben paused at the door. The fat man looked up in surprise. "I've read all your books. I kind of like them."

Hours had passed in the room; but not in the waiting corridor outside. Four pairs of eyes turned to him as he came through the door in the loosely wrapped bathrobe, clothes bundled under his arm.

"Thank god," muttered the man in the black suit. "Literature marches on again."

The agent waved a polaroid camera. "Great. Let's get it all recorded."

"What about my money?" said Ben.

She frowned. "Oh alright." She crooked a finger at the man in the black suit, who took money from his inside breast pocket, counted out a handful of notes and passed them over. "Now can we get this over with?"

"Yeah sure, but, like I'm really dying for a pee. I was stuck in there for ages."

"Should have done it on Cowper," muttered the man in the black suit. "I'm sure he wouldn't have minded."

The agent glared at him, turned to Ben. "Just make it quick."

In the cramped yellowish washroom Ben pissed at his own murky reflection in a battered steel urinal. He looked badly beaten, his skin turned indigo from neck to knees.

He studied himself in the cracked mirror over the handbasin. Mirror-writing crossed his chest. Discarding his robe, he climbed onto the sink to get a better view.

LET MY TONGUE
EXPLORE YOU
GENTLY. LET THIS STRANGE
CONTINENT BE
MET WITH LOVE
AND PILLAGE. I
DREAM OF A
TONGUE LONG
ENOUGH TO
WORK ITS WAY
INSIDE YOU ALL
THE WAY TO LICK
YOUR WARM
INTERIOR, A
BUTTERFLY
TONGUE.

For a moment he squatted there, thinking of his clothes out in the corridor, his favourite red sweater; then jumped down and recounted the money from the bathrobe pocket.

The window was small and stiff on its hinges. He forced it open and had a view down to the river through a tangle of iron fire-escapes.

Ben picked his way back across the city, through shadows, down back alleys and across walls, hiding from pedestrians and cars, darting quickly across roads as far between streetlamps as he could manage. Once he thought he saw the agent's car screech fast around a distant corner.

If anybody saw him, any bag person rousing from an alcoholic doze, any roadie flyposting for their band, any clubber or bouncer, any security guard or night cleaner or insomniac or cop; then they must have thought him a dream or a ghost, fleet across the night.

By the time he got back to his squat the horizon was bleached with the dirty acid glow of sunrise. Wolf, asleep with his head on the table in a citadel of empty bottles, woke with a start, looked up and laughed. "What the fuck happened to you?"

"It's a long story." Ben grinned. "–Or a chapter at least."

Come the morning yawning open and Lizette scratched her head and yawned with it. She unlocked the front door and found a kid already hanging around on the doorstep. "Early start," she grumbled. "So what'll it be? Rose? Skull? Not, I hope, another fucking bimbo with monster tits."

He shook his head and opened his shirt.

She whistled and bent over to see it better. "You got this stuff all over?"

"Yeah."

"Cute," she said. "It'll take time. And money."

"I haven't got a lot," he said and showed her. "Money I mean; I've got plenty of time."

"This isn't a charity," said Lizette but took the cash. "What the fuck. It'll make a change. Come into my parlour."

The needle traced the same path as the pen, but in fire. Ben worried he might get used to pain, might even get a liking for it. "I don't need that shit," he told himself: but from beginning to end it only hurt.

On the last day the tattooist asked, "Going to look for a job in a circus?" as she packed the gear away.

He lay in agony on the old dentist's chair. "Don't think so," he mumbled.

On the last day the tattooist asked, "Going to look for a job in a circus?" as she packed the gear away.

He lay in agony on the old dentist's chair. "Don't think so," he mumbled.

"Guess that's not the only line of work where it might be useful."

"Guess not."

It took a couple of weeks before he was healed up and could sleep a whole night through without pills. A couple of days later he was crossing a bridge when a car kerbcrawled alongside and the window zipped down.

"Did you think that was funny?" demanded the agent. "What is it, you hate art or something? You think it's a joke to throw away somebody's work like that?"

"Have you got my clothes?" Ben asked. "The red jumper?"

"Fuck your rags," said the agent. "I burned them. Oxfam are fussier than that. Where's my money? Get in the car."

"I didn't hate what he wrote," said Ben. "I thought it was pretty good."

"Spare me your critical insights— Wait! You mean you took a copy?" Ben opened his shirt and showed her. For a moment the agent was speechless; then she roared, "Your body is in breach of copyright, you little shit!"

Ben gave her the finger. He ran along the bridge and jumped down the steps to the embankment while the car was still jerking to a halt at the top. In a minute he was lost among concrete pillars on the underside.

Nine months passed and the weather turned round to winter. Going past a bookshop Ben noticed a fat cardboard cutout leering from the window. He went in and found a stack of new books in a display stand by the counter. On the cover was a murky matt photo of a naked boy twisting through air. It was titled **LIKE MAYBE**. He leafed through. Where chapter 16 should have been he found half a dozen blank pages.

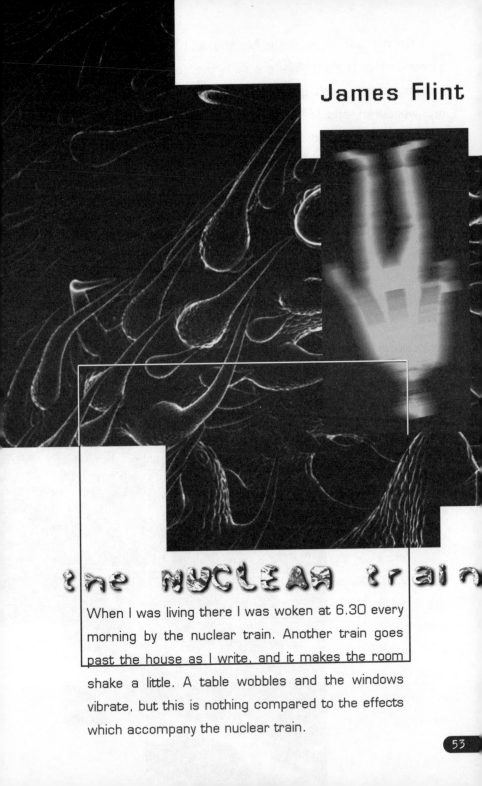

James Flint

the NUCLEAR train

When I was living there I was woken at 6.30 every morning by the nuclear train. Another train goes past the house as I write, and it makes the room shake a little. A table wobbles and the windows vibrate, but this is nothing compared to the effects which accompany the nuclear train.

On my last night there Martha and Mary lay in the bath together, fully clothed. "I've got no arms," said Martha, shrieking with laughter. "I can't get out, I've got no arms." I watched them and wondered, should I turn on the taps? What stopped me, I'm not sure, but it had to do with Mary's eyes which I felt on me even though her head was turned away.

A little later I thought: *I worry about my health. Tonight I am going to rob the health store. I have it all planned. I'll get Dmitri, with the long eyelashes and beautiful Roman nose, to help. He will be an asset if there are women or queers involved. Me—I'm too ugly. But I know that, I accept it. My beauty lies in my skill with appliances and in the fact that I know when to keep quiet, and when to talk.*

Here's the plan. We'll disable the alarm with sodabread and stuff our loot into raffia bags woven in hospitals by invalids.

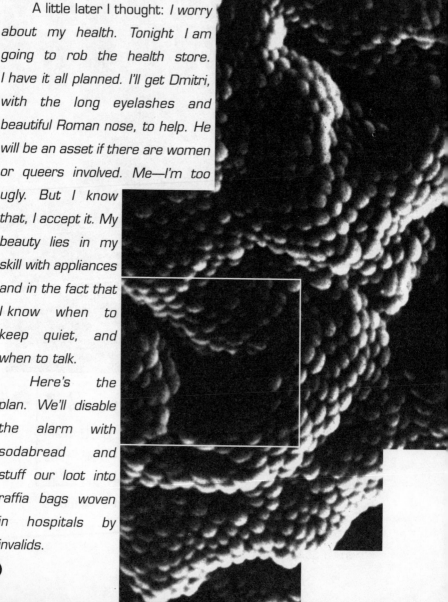

We'll smoke yage and shoot anyone who gets in our way and trash the place. Dmitri can shit in the cashtill; it's more his thing than mine. Then we'll leave together for Docklands and hide from the law amongst the taxis, the battleships and the foam.

Rever lurked there already, in a Portacabin by a satellite dish. Rever is quite mad. He had a dog once but he lost it down one of the many holes that have been sunk ready to take the piles for the skyscrapers. On clear days he climbs the cranes and the gantrys and calls for his dog across this land which is sodden earth and filthy water and whole worlds of garbage in between. This ground beneath our feet is riddled with stinking air. Rever says that when he's up high he can watch the wavelets in the square docks shimmer and mix as they pad down the heaving numbers that permutate beneath them.

Rever became sick, and we gave him pills that we had stolen from the shop. Dmitri took some too, for good measure; he'd lost a lot of fluid. I was far away but still I could feel Mary's eyes just like that last night of decision.

Down here the days bleed into one another. We spend our time, now as then, picking amongst the rubbish piles that punctuate the waterfront, each heap a lazy full stop on the useful life of consumables: rotting food, packaging, glass and bricks and mortar, bones and the carcasses of white goods. I would like to say that I found something poignant, like the juxtaposition of a child's doll and an umbrella, or a bundle of love letters lying in the bruised petals from a old bouquet, or even yet a hat, a pipe, the racing pages. All these things were there of course, but they carried no weight at all, no nostalgia. The garbage here no longer resonates with the past. I complained at this, said I missed my home, with its noise and smells and three inches of subsidence that showed on all three floors, but Rever told me that I was foolish, that I had no right, that down here things were moving on and that I should be grateful for this horn of plenty that brought us objects freed from connotations.

This did not satisfy me, it meant nothing to me. I nagged at him; I told him that I worried for Martha, that I missed her, that she couldn't survive down here because she had no arms, and eventually he gave way to my sentimentality and said he'd help me build her some, from turntables and the guts of several washing machines. I embarked upon this project with glee, and felt no guilt at all in enlisting Rever's aid for several hours each day, because every morning after all he'd been forcing the rest of us to search for his wretched dog, which he claimed beyond all reason was still alive and roaming through the earth beneath us, foraging for light and air and living off moles and worms.

But I didn't hear from Martha as she had promised although Mary's eyes still haunted me at night. Soon I began to lose heart in the arms and they lay twitching in a pool of oil with no one to attend to them. I feared the worst—that the two of them had been implicated in the theft and taken in for questioning. I thought that any contact might be dangerous, but this subtracted the aim from all my designs of a new life on the waterfront. As I had not yet learnt just how big the tides around me were I could see little point in the day to day and became listless. My behaviour infuriated my companions, who soon would not let me near the fire at night. I wasn't pulling my weight on the rubbish heaps, but I could not see the point in salvage once the aim of the operation—preparing for the girls' arrival—had been denied me. The detritus on the heaps had no connotations in the first place; to work with it at all I felt

I had to be allowed to impose my own. Now even this had been denied me, and for the first time I began to regret the actions which had brought me here.

Again it was Rever who saved me.

I think now that he had been watching me all along, aware of my course and watching it run. Whether that's the case or not, at one point he took me aside and walked alone with me along a jetty.

"If you want to find them, why don't you search in there?" he said, and motioned towards the cluster of towers that stood in the middle distance and dominated the skyline and the red night.

"What is there that would help me?" I asked.

"Don't you know?"

"No idea."

"That which you see is the conduit for all the information. The tallest building is a processor. Not long ago, there were many small operations, doing the job in their own fashion, dotted around the city. And then they built this. Most of the old ones have been replaced. Nearly all the information gets channelled through here now. That's why I came here. I wanted to experience the reorganisation of these flows."

I looked at the buildings and I looked at the docks that had been let into the earth before them. I looked anywhere except at Rever's haggard face, charred with old memories of knife fights and acne. I watched a frigate maneouvring its stern out from the pier. It turned, and entered the lock which was massive, twice its size. Looking at the helipads and I dreamt for a moment of sonar and radar interfering with my body. I thought of a room filled with bronzes. It was a place I had never been. Later, I did what Rever said, and visited the building.

I'm told—by Rever, of course—that the nuclear train comes down here to unload. I think I saw it as I picked my way across the scrub and mud flats towards the building. Black as night and twice as long. I thought: this is my only connection with home. I thought of home, my old home, the home before the one I have now: *There is a sausage factory two doors down. You can't see the factory from the street—it's in a back room and lets out only on the train line, where the rats dance, drunk with isotopes. But from our* bathroom you can see the workers stuffing guts with sausage meat for hours and hours. We have a story we tell about how they make the sausages from rats, and feed them to the children who are bad. It frightens us more than the children. But the word has got around and the neighbours are beginning to shun us.

You can tell the nuclear train by its weight. Most trains, the passenger trains, the goods trains, they rattle the windows and cause liquid to oscillate in cups. But the nuclear train rocks the whole building to and fro with a deep rhythm, and the house settles down and down into its foundations. They replaced the street out front a month ago, and already there is another small crater. Everything round here is falling apart.

I told Mary about the rats that danced, the sausages and the neighbours, the craters and the train. These were the everyday, there was not a problem. But when I told her about her eyes she left the room and looked at me. A vase fell off the shelf, which I caught. I put it back and went to the window to look for trains. I yelled at Mary to come back and she did, and I told her about the vase and she said it made sense what with the things she was learning to do with her head.

"What sort of things?" I asked. I was worried.

"Oh, you know, moving things and that."

"What sort of things?" She demonstrated, shyly, and to change the subject, by rattling a glass until it fell from the table to the floor. She was standing by the sink, which is not near the table. I picked it up and went to the window to look for trains.

"But there are no trains now."

"Yes," she said, somewhat enigmatically. I asked if this was a recent development. I did not know what to say. But Mary could not—or would not—remember. I got progressively more angry with the challenge posed by all of this and would become frustrated and vent my rage around the apartment.

"I feel sick, I feel so sick sick sick!" I would scream, hitting the wall. I developed denial. I told Mary I thought it was the nuclear train, that it was making me ill, that something would have to be done, and she told me that yes, she agreed. But I could tell by the look in her eyes when I slept that she knew I would be going away. I didn't want to go I told her, but I had to. I made her promise to follow me, and bring Martha too, and we'd start a new life, away from here. But I got the feeling that my words were by no means new to her.

So I robbed the health store with Dmitri and we came down here to hide. And Martha and Mary never followed, even though I built the arms and came to understand the nuclear train in the end. I did look for them in the building like Rever suggested, and though once I found a photograph there was nothing I could piece together. But by then it was okay, I wasn't so bothered, because I'd come to understand that the way it had been before was not the way things worked and that all these things had come to me not I to them. And in those last days in that building, in the run up to the moment when my access was finally denied, I knew from my position on the eighteenth floor exactly where Rever was at all times, and the position of his dog, too, deep there beneath us, in the wormholes of the earth. And so when I left it was no longer a problem for me, and I returned to the salvage with the others, and I worked at it without past, without future, and I knew the objects that I needed when I saw them, even though there was neither nostalgia nor connotation amongst them. And I am with Mary, like now when I write, even though she is not here, and I know she is

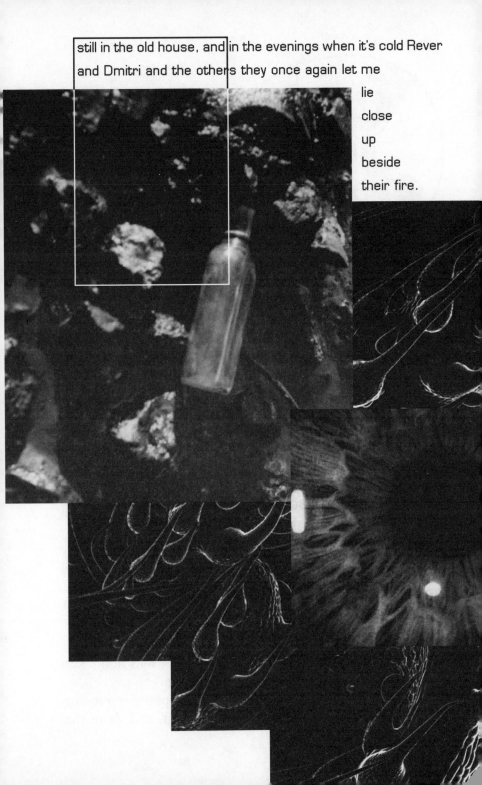

still in the old house, and in the evenings when it's cold Rever
and Dmitri and the others they once again let me

lie

close

up

beside

their fire.

Pepsi

Matthew Barro

A man walks into a corner shop and buys a crate of fifty Pepsi cans. The cans are wet and icy, fresh from the shores of America itself. They stand gleaming in the centre of the shop. The man stares at them and licks his lips.

The shopkeeper leans his elbows on the counter.

"As you can see, signor, they have arrived. Will it please you to take them now or have them delivered?"

The man looks at the shopkeeper out of the corner of his eye and rubs his upper lip, grinning.

"Now," he says. "I'll take them now."

"Very good, signor."

The shopkeeper punches something into his till.

"That will be fifteen quid."

The man nods, impatient, not listening; and then recovering his senses, he reaches into his pocket and pulls out two grubby notes. He shoves them hard into the shopkeeper's hand.

"Keep the change, brother," he tells him. "Keep the change."

The shopkeeper puts the money away and slams the

till shut. It rings and rattles.

"How will signor be moving it?" he asks. "If I may inquire."

But the man is already rolling up his sleeves and striding forward, stretching his arms towards the ceiling and taking deep breaths. He squats down before the crate and shuffles his fingertips under it. In a single motion he lifts it up, standing upright in a perfect textbook manner, back straight, bending only at the knee.

The shopkeeper claps his hands in delight.

"Signor, that was masterful! Masterful!"

"Open the door!" the man commands.

The shopkeeper runs around and opens the door. Above their heads the little bell rings clear and loud. The man steps out into the glare of a blue and sunny sky. On either side of him stretch endless rows of terraced houses. The streets are bare. He takes a second step forward. A small gust of wind brushes his cheek and pushes a strand of hair across his forehead. He frowns. He looks back towards the shop but the door has closed. He looks left and right, serious and suspicious. Another gust of wind brushes across the back of his head. He jumps.

"Jesus Christ," he growls.

He drops the crate on the ground and tears the coat from his back to cover the cans. Two gusts of wind, one from the left and one from the right smack into either side of the Pepsis. A loud, echoing THWAK! belts through the street. He moans and falls to his knees.

The Pepsi cans struck by the wind, split and shatter. Some explode, some just bend double and leak. In a single split second, the whole crate is ruined. Black Pepsi runs around his knees and soaks his jeans, spills over the side of the kerb and onto the road. He touches it. It's still fizzing, like the nerves of a still twitching corpse.

He touches his fingers to his lips.

At the centre of the crate, a single can, crumpled and misshapen, remains intact. When another gust of wind shifts the pile, it falls from its hiding place and rolls in a mutilated, pitiful way until it comes to rest before his knees. He looks at the can for some time before he realizes that it has not leaked. He picks it up and holds it above his head, turning it in his hands, examining it in the sunlight. If it didn't have Pepsi written on it, bent double at least fourteen times, it would hardly be recognisable as a can at all. Bringing it down, he pulls it open. There's a burst of gas, but no foam. He holds it above his mouth and tips it: nothing. He shakes it. Nothing. He stands up and examines it again.

"Jesus Christ," he growls. This has happened only once before in his lifetime, more than twenty years ago, when he was a boy. In those days the only thing to do was to put it down to experience. Accept your lot. Today, he knows how to make the enemy work for him; how to harness that power which harms you and use it to serve your own needs.

"Wind is neither good nor evil!" he tells himself. "That which it destroys it can also repair."

He walks until he comes to a multi-crossroads, a concrete island in its centre. The roads are quiet. He crosses to the island without pausing at the kerb. The Pepsi can protected in his hands, he walks to each of the three corners of the island. He licks his finger and tests the air for speed and direction. Satisfied, he stands in the centre of the island, his feet exactly two foot apart, positioning his hands at different heights in front of him. When he finds the ideal height—about the height of his chest—he stands motionless, the can still covered in his fist, and waits.

Every car that passes, from whatever direction, he watches it like a hawk. He turns from left to right, craning to see behind him, to see just what is coming from where. After fifteen minutes, he spies a red car coming from behind him to his right, a blue car coming towards him to his left. Mouth open, he turns to see what is coming at him from his extreme right, and sure enough he sees a white van.

"Hallelujah!" he screams,

and releases the can from his smothering hands. The cars pass him one at a time, each whizzing by, first the blue, then the white, then the red, each dragging air behind it... air that bounces off the other's air, and spins, and meets and crashes in the middle—where the Pepsi can, already beaten and mutilated, now gets buffeted, battered and flattened... pushed and pulled this way and that, in and out of shape, so that finally, when the wind has passed and the air is still, the can is a cylinder again: smooth if scarred, upright if dented, restored to its original shape. A proper can.

The man holds it aloft in his right hand and pours black Pepsi into his mouth. "Not today," he chuckles and laughs aloud, alone on the island.

about the authors...

Eroica Mildmay (**Electricccccccccccccccity**) wrote the novel *Lucker and Tiffany peel out* (Serpent's Tail) and is currently completing a second novel. **Fashion victims** is Adam Wishart's first published fiction and yes he has been known to read *blah blah blah*. **Birchsap** author Volha Ipatava is a creature of controversy in her home country, Belarus; many of her poems have been translated into English by Vera Rich (as was this story); she also publishes the magazine *Kultura*. Laura Pachkowski's **This land is our land** was destined for *The Living Room*, but spent some time lost in cyberspace. Amy Prior, who wrote **Angel on the rooftops**, used to do a problem page on a lipsticks and facelifts magazine. Emma Kate Martin (**Aliens**) lives in New Zealand's South Island, so how she heard about Pulp Faction is kind of mysterious. Michael River was once shipwrecked on Madagascar... **Like maybe.** James Flint (**Nuclear train**) works in London. Matthew Barrow has written several weird tales besides **Pepsi** in which the everyday collides with the paranormal. Nicholas Royle's story **Get a half life** is a sequel to **City of Fusion** (*Technopagan*); his novels *Counterparts* and *Saxophone Dreams* are published by Penguin. Jonathon Staines (**Wideboys**) feels safer scuba-diving in shark infested seas than back home in Essex. **Mea glck mo ments** is Jamie Jackson's first published fiction, but what he really wants to do is direct films...hey Jamie, don't we all? Duncan Brown (**Apocalypse now and then**) quit his job as bass player with Stereolab to write; another of his stories is in the punk anthology *Gobbing, Pogoing and Gratuitous Bad Language*. Carol Swain, author of **Soft concrete**, also had a graphic novel published recently. Jay Welsh (**Meat**) is working on a screenplay about smalltime suburban sadism. Alistair Gentry wrote **Teen lite**. Simon Miles (**The Sniper**) is involved in occasional literary event *The Cupboard Club*. Finally, thanks to Craig Yamey for this picture. —*Elaine Palmer (editor)*

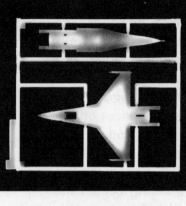

nicholas royle

Get a
HALF
LIFE

After her second trip to see Jim Cover, art director to out-twat all other art directors, Lilith was on a high. A natural high. And all she needed from André was that he show some pleasure, that he share her success just a little bit, instead of making her feel small, instead of undermining her yet again. Instead of making his own spurious moral judgments on the magazines she wanted to work for.

"Don't you understand?" she'd said to him before heading into town. "It's not who I *want* to work for, it's who I *have* to work for, if I want to get on. It's like, how can you expect to be taken seriously as a writer unless you've appeared in *Granta*? Or how do you think you'll ever make it big as an artist unless you're mentioned in the same paragraph as Damien fucking Hirst. You know? I've gotta be in *Details*. I've gotta be in *Don't Tell It*. And *Ray Gun* and *iD* and *Blah Blah Blah*. Until I am, I've got no cred."

"It's just one big fucking circus," he opined, screwing up his weaselly face as he sucked all the goodness out of one of his characteristically slender spliffs. "You wanna climb on board, fine. Just don't expect me to applaud."

"Why do you have to be like this?"

He destroyed the spliff in the ashtray. "Born like it? I dunno."

So after the second interview, when Jim Cover went for her random shoot in such a big way she could see the very next thing he was going to do was commission her, she half dreaded André would bring her down. And yet, it was thanks to him in a way that she'd got the amber light with Jim Cover. If he hadn't explained how to foresee the future by discerning patterns in randomly scattered soil...if he hadn't introduced her to the ad industry types who hosted the party in Bateman Street at which, up a rusty fire escape to a Cocteau Twins soundtrack, she fused

earth and sky...if he hadn't made sure she was sorted, that night of all nights...she might never have spawned the idea for the shoot: random styles thrown together within different genre conventions. That's what the random distribution of earth showed her. And Jim Cover was convinced enough to commission her. She knew it. She *knew* it.

"André," she called, slamming the front door. "Are you there?"

He had to be, the door had only been single-locked.

She found him where she'd left him, slumped on the kitchen floor, stoned out of his box. The ashtray held half a dozen dead roaches. Bending down to get a good look at him, she grasped his jaw and shook it just about enough, she thought, to wake him. But he didn't move. She called his name a couple of times, slapped his cheek. Nothing. She reached into the side pocket of his Dutch Army fatigues where he usually kept a little tin of downers. The tin was there but when she shook it she heard nothing.

"Fuck."

She checked to see if he had a pulse. He did. Just.

She stood up and leant against the work surface, folding her arms across her chest. She looked at him. His legs splayed, boots scuffed, body bent forward at the waist. One arm draped in his lap, the other lining up with the skirting board. He'd bought the army fatigues in a surplus store in Cork on a trip they'd made together. The babe top was Duffer of St George, the silver socks from Kensington Market. She attached mental price tags to the items, visualised a DPS, even gave it a head—Drugs Duds.

She considered getting her camera out, taking a few shots, but plugged in the coffee maker instead. A cup of strong black joe and he'd be on his feet. She had to pour it into his mouth, dribbles escaping down his neck. The shock roused him, spluttering and coughing, to demand what the fuck was going on. She merely pointed at the ashtray and stalked out, wishing for the nth time she could afford a place of her own. Relying on the charity of a misogynistic junkhead for affection and accommodation was hardly ideal. Lilith had been assisting for a still-lifer who did stuff for Jim Cover but the fucker had blown her out when he heard she'd been lugging her own portfolio up to Cover's eighth-floor eyrie.

"I'm not competing with you," she'd attempted to explain to him over the phone. "I'm not even doing still lifes, so how can I be?"

"Look, love..." there was a pause while he downshifted and negotiated a junction—he'd called her from the car, on his way down to Nine Elms to pick up some cheap rostrum gear, so he'd said. "If all the time you're assisting me you're thinking about your own work and maybe even how *you'd* light what *I'm* shooting, then your mind's not on the game, you know, and I need someone who's there for me. A hundred and ten per cent. No part-timers in this game, love. Yeah? I'll have to let you go." She'd hung up before he could wish her good luck in her new career.

Yeah, fuck you too, asshole.

When André came to bed that night he was maudlin, thanked her for helping him out, kissing her hands, pawing her tits. She turned to face the window.

Jim Cover rang the next day. Ten past nine. André cursed and pulled the duvet over his shaggy head as Lilith scooped up the handset and copped a load of the art director's early morning energy.

"Yeah, so, Lilith. You wanna do a piece? I wanna give you an assignment, but I wanna leave it pretty much up to you, yeah? Give me a good location. That's important. Night shots'd be cool, long exposures, fancy stuff, whatever. Give me something no one else could, yeah? I think that's your strength. Next Tuesday, yeah? Something street. Rough 'n' ready. Otherwise up to you."

"Yeah, right."

He'd gone.

Next Tuesday. After the weekend on the coast with André and his friends. Was there time? Of course there was. She'd make time.

She jumped up and ran round the room, leaping off the floor, bouncing on the bed.

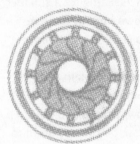

"I got it, I got it, I got it," she yelled. "I got it, André. I got a commission."

"Fuck off," came his muffled reply.

She stood still, panting, sweat beading on the sides of her delicate nose.

"Well, fuck you, André," she shouted. "Fuck you, fuck you, fuck you!"

She picked up the first thing she saw—his Army trousers—and hurled them at the shape under the duvet.

He couldn't even be bothered to grunt.

She grabbed her stuff and headed for the bathroom.

The nearest decent-sized newsagent was a couple of miles away by the Tube, but that was okay because she needed time to think. André's place was far enough out from the centre of town that the streets were fairly empty—ideal conditions just to let her mind go. The random shoot apart, all Lilith's best ideas had come to her on the way to the Tube. And if the idea came early enough, she then had plenty of time to plot the rest. What clothes she'd use on what sort of models and against what background. The theme was the idea that came in the first place. Now she needed a new one for the commission. There'd been a glimmer of an idea in the kitchen the night before when she'd had a good look at André before waking him up. The Drugs Duds thing. But she wasn't sure.

She didn't understand André. It wasn't that he didn't care about fashion, he did. You only had to look at his labels. The clothes looked shit on him but that was his fault, the way he wore them.

She *had* thought that André might have been one of the links, or might have been able to help her find them.

When her mother had died, Lilith had been cast adrift at the age of 16, her father having fucked off long ago, emigrated to Seattle by all

 accounts while still young. Grieving, she'd sought comfort in the things that she perceived as being links between one part of the world and the next. She was only trying to hold her life together.

"It's like a string bag that's coming undone and I'm trying not to lose all my oranges out of it," she'd explained to her counsellor.

"What you need to try to do," he began, "is look for the links between one part of your life and the next, and when you've found them, look after them. Be pleased that they are there—because they *are* there, it's just a matter of finding them—and then nurture them. It sounds easy, Lilith, and it *is* easy. You will not prosper in isolation. Do not think that because your father left and your mother died you will forever be left to fend for yourself. Likewise the different parts of your life, and the different things going on in the world. They're all interdependent. If things get desperate, just find those links and hold on to them."

So when she met André and he was going on about bringing together the earth and the sky to create the geomancer's city of fusion, she went for that stuff. She took it right in. And it worked in so far as she came up with the random shoot idea for Jim Cover, and so around we go. The new commission. Her first. She needed something big, something strong. Something to make them sit up and take notice. Her byline was going to be 'Lilith'. Just that. No surname. Lilith.

André could have been the link between her emotional life and her professional life, if he'd given more of a fuck about her work, and if he'd been capable of feeling anything more profound than the need, indeed, to fuck.

She scanned the shelves in the Minimart, took down *Marie Claire, Elle, Vogue, Sky* and a few others. She wasn't going to buy them, she couldn't afford to—she saved all her cash for Ektachrome these days—just have a leaf through to see what they were doing on their fashion pages, so that she could see what *not* to do. She wanted to go beyond them all. She wanted to do something extreme. Body piercing and scarification and branding had been done to death.

There was a model in *Sky* looked like André: the unshaven juvenile beard, the same insolent leer. She'd asked André several times if she could shoot him. She'd flattered him, told him he was a natural, but he just pouted even more and turned away. Once she sneaked up on him and snapped a couple before he knew what she was doing, but he ripped the camera off her and exposed the film. "Spoilt get," she'd muttered, rubbing her hand where his nails had left red marks.

When she got back to the flat it was to find all her stuff slung out in the hall, not even packed into bags.

"You fucker!" she screamed, banging on the door with her fists.

There was no point. He'd gone out.

André had faults but total stupidity wasn't one of them. He knew that *she* knew that if he'd hung around he'd have ended up opening the door to her. She sank to her knees in the draughty hallway.

It was a Thursday. The plan for the weekend had been to join some friends in a small seaside hotel. Friends of André's, but they'd become friends of hers as well. The truth was she was brighter than André. He could compute as fast as a PowerMac but had little imagination. His friends were more creative—writers, artists, a mad sculptor—and Lilith felt at ease with them. It would piss André off no end, but that was tough.

"Hey Lilith."

"Hi."

"Lilith. Hi, how's it going?"

"Hey, what's up?"

Laughter.

Whispering: "What the hell's she doing here?"

"Lilith, how're you doing?"

"She's not. Where?"

"Over there, talking to Kelvin."

"Lilith?"

"Tracey! How did your thing go? You know, your show?"

"She can't be. I kicked her out. She wouldn't dare show up."

"She's over there, asshole. Looks like you didn't kick her out hard enough."

"Darling. Lovely to see ya. Didn't you...I thought you and André...you know..."

"Yeah. I came on my own. Doesn't mean I can't continue to see you guys, does it. I was invited. I figured the invitation was still open."

"Absolutely, darling. But, look, oh I'm really sorry."

"Yeah, well. You know..."

"Is that...? André's gonna be fucking chuffed to the tits. *Not.* Christ, she's got a nerve. Has he seen her yet?"

"He's over there."

"Well, you know, I've been looking forward to this weekend for some time. And I just got my first real commission, so I thought I'd come and celebrate. I gather it should be quite a night."

"You bet. Kelvin's raided the pharmacy. We are *stocked.*"

"Cheers."

"Cheers."

"Hello André."

"Christ."

"You can either act civil or be a cunt. Depends what you want your friends to think of you."

"What the fuck are you doing here?"

"So you're going to be a cunt. The invite had my name on it. Get used to it."

Every summer Kelvin booked this small hotel on the Suffolk coast. Booked it solid and invited whoever he wanted to invite. He paid for everything. It was his present to himself and to all his friends. Kelvin had made it big in conceptual art despite never being one of the Damien Hirst set. He'd never exhibited at White Cube or met Jay Jopling, but he'd sold a couple of pieces to the Saatchis and had a sell-out show at New York's Cohen Gallery. New York loved him. The *Voice* ran an eight-page interview, *Time Out New York* made it its cover star, the *Times* notice was an embarrassment of superlatives. Out on the Suffolk coast, Kelvin enjoyed the anonymity.

Lilith didn't feel bad about coming along after the bust-up with André. Kelvin wasn't short of a bob or two and her name *had* been on the invite.

Wilma sashayed back from the bar and thrust a Bud into Lilith's hand.

"Get that down ya neck, girl," she commanded as she straightened her garish skull cap. "So tell me about this commission. I mean that's brilliant news. What happened?"

"Oh they just got fed up of me pestering them, you know. Gave me something to do just to get rid of me. But tell me about your sculpture. How's it going?"

"Oh well you know, beating the shit out o' a massive slab o' granite—beats having a relationship. It doesnae answer back and I get fuckin paid fer it. I'm tellin ya, it's great. Here..."

"Already?" Lilith took the pill from Wilma's hand.

"Aye. Why not. Might as well get started. We're no the only ones."

And when Lilith looked round she could see several glowing brows, a few sets of dilated pupils. She clocked André at the far side of the bar hunched in his seat and scowling as he bitched about her to Darren, whose habit made André's look amateurish; while Lilith watched, he was cutting up a couple of lines on the table top with his Gold Card. André's eyes glittered greedily. She looked at what he was wearing—it would do.

Her cameras were upstairs. She'd worked it with the desk clerk so she had a single room.

"Are you ready?"

"I will be in a minute. Just got to get my camera."

Kelvin carried a ghetto blaster on the walk down to the beach. The hotel was only a quarter mile from the sea but the party was heading north across a patch of mixed marsh and scrubland before turning right to hit the path to the beach. Strung out along the winding path, the group looked less like an Outward Bound course than a school field trip in mufti. It was already past 8.30, getting on for nine o'clock, and the shadows in among the juniper and gorse were beginning to knit together.

Lilith strained to make out shapes and faces: it was what she loved most about E.

"Are you getting anything?" she asked Wilma. "I'm getting flashing lights. Little green lights at the edge of my vision."

"That's no the drugs, darlin. That's the glow-worms."

"What? No!"

"Aye. Take a look. Next one you see, get down and check it out. Aye, check these out as well while you're at it." She rummaged in her pocket, produced a little plastic wallet.

"Mushies!"

"Taste like shit so swallow 'em wi' lots and lots o' beer."

Lilith didn't need a diagram.

The E was coming on. Creeping up on her, rather than rushing. Out of the corner of her eye she caught sight of another glow-worm. She dropped to her hands and knees.

"I'll catch you up."

"Don't get lost."

It was like the anti-counterfeit stuff they'd started putting on concert tickets. Hold it to the light and it goes green. Change the angle and it's silver again. As she moved, the glow-worm disappeared, then was back again, glowing a soft, sleepy green. She reached through the undergrowth and delicately picked it up, rolled it in the palm of her hand, now glistening with sweat. No longer than her thumbnail, it curled up but still glowed. She put it back, the E rushing now. She rolled over in the scrub. Heather and bracken brushed her cheek soft as down. Grasshoppers chirruped. When she peered back into the little bush where she'd found the glow-worm, there it was, still glowing. Only now it was *really* glowing. A small luminescent globe hung suspended within the little bush. Its light travelled for miles across the marsh towards the sea, which Lilith could hear as a faint susurration somewhere behind her. She rolled over again then jumped up and sprang on to her hands, her legs twisting effortlessly in the dusky air. Green lights flew around her head as she performed cartwheels and somersaults.

She lay panting in the grass several yards from where she'd seen the glow-worm. Her hands were glowing now, unfeasibly pink and clean. A fine film of sweat covered her brow. She scanned the vegetation around her and wherever she looked tiny green eyes stared back into hers.

How long had she been lying there? She knew she mustn't get left behind. Above all, she had a shoot to do. She jumped up and found her camera by the first bush.

They were down on the beach already. She was sorry to leave the scrubland—as she trod delicately across its margin she heard all the tiniest creatures calling out to her, watched the long grasses feathering in the warm breeze—but the others had got a fire going on the beach and already she could spy little faces dancing among the flames. A man on a motorbike throttled hard from in the thick of the fire, his hands steady on his flickering handlebars of flame. A tiger shot out from the top of the fire into the weirdly luminescent sky above— beyond the fire and half a mile or so down the beach was the nuclear power station. Then she saw André round the other side of the fire and for a moment felt she could forgive him, but then she snatched at that feeling and screwed it up and threw it in the flames. His eyes were fucked. She didn't know what he was on, and nor did she want to. Someone had fallen asleep with her feet only six inches or so from the edge of the fire where the soles of her boots had melted and she'd obviously been kicking her legs around in her sleep—her Sue Engels cushioned-heel casual boots were like two big Toffee Crisps, dozens of pebbles fused into the crepe soles.

Well worth a few snap-snap-snaps.

So what if it was out of focus, overexposed, if her hands were shaking so much, her fingers so slippery the pics ended up like French Impressionists—the last thing fashion editors were interested in was making out the gear. That's what the captions were for. As long as something got captioned and it cost a fuck of a lot, you knew you'd done your job. And the fashion victims snapped their Visa cards down on another King's Road counter.

"Darlin'."

Lilith hugged Wilma, almost dropping her camera in the fire.

"Don't do that," Wilma chided. "Come wi' me. I want tae show ya something."

And as Lilith followed Wilma down the beach, the mushies finally strapped themselves into the driving seat and put their foot down. The power station hovered just above the ground up ahead, but the problem was the sea. The sea, on her left, had suddenly reared up into a vertical wall of steel; grey, shiny and uneven, made out of beaten panels, like the side of a locomotive. It still made sea noises but it wasn't spread out flat any more, like the sea was supposed to be.

"Wilms, Wilms."

"Excuse me if I don't walk alongside you," Wilma was shouting back happily. "But some fucker's laid out an entire fucking restaurant of tables and chairs here on the beach, and I'm having to dodge them as I go."

Pretty fucking reasonable from where Lilith was standing.

They both walked on, at their different paces, coping with their respective obstacles. The power station hummed in the distance and never seemed to get any closer.

"What do you want to show me? Wilms. *Jesus!!* Look at the sky!"

The sky was a screen. Faces slithered across it like a montage sequence in a film, faces she knew, faces she'd never seen before but felt comfortable with, faces she could never have imagined in a million years.

"Jesus Christ, these are good fucking drugs."

In case anyone was in any doubt.

Wilma shouted above the din of the restaurant in her head: "Look at that fucker!"

And Lilith turned away from the train, which had now become a tunnel, a steel-walled tunnel in a booming railway station, towards the land, to see that they had finally come alongside the power station.

It was huge. An enormous humming beast, sleek and shiny, softly glowing. It was hard to believe that inside such a beautiful behemoth, men in white coats went whizzing round on unicycles juggling spent fuel rods.

A thought entered her head. A line from nowhere.

Where did the inspiration for the look come from?

The splitting of an atomic nucleus into approximately equal parts, with an associated release of energy.

Approximately. *Approximately!* There was no approximately about it. How could she have ever thought that splitting up with André would destroy her? Would do her anything but good? How could she have been so dumb? This wasn't just drugs. (Yeah, it was mainly drugs, but not *just* drugs.) This was about release, release of energy. That fucker had kept her locked up in his own little world too long, far too long. She felt like a pit bull terrier that had spent a year running round and round on a hamster wheel. And now the door to the cage had been left open.

"Wilms, Wilms," she shouted above the spaceship buzz of the power station, loud enough to pierce the clatter of Wilma's tables and chairs. And she started to run back, grabbing her camera to keep it safe.

"Lilith, where're you going?"

"Follow me. I've got my feature," she called over her shoulder. "I've got my shoot."

She waited for Wilma to catch up, then stood on tiptoes and brought her face close to her friend's. Gazed into her eyes. Saw nothing but her own reflection.

Before she was aware of it, she was running away again, arms wheeling, down to the sea, where she kicked up spray like a shower of sparks, then she flopped like a rag doll in a drama class warm-up. *Okay, two, three and...drop. You're a rag doll. Drop from the waist.* She stared into the curling waves and moved her head slowly from side to side.

Yes, there they were; whether she kept her head still or moved it around, they were still there. Little green lights in the water. Little green maggoty things, surfing the gentle breakers and vanishing in the undertow. Lilith bent further down, peering closer, entranced.

"Glow-worms," she whispered.

"No darlin'. Phosphorescence."

Wilma was beside her.

"Drugs?" she asked. "Look, there's another one."

"No." Wilma shook her head, almost losing her skull cap.

"Phosphorescence. They live in the sea. You only see them at night."

"But they're like the glow-worms."

"They're different."

"They're fucking brilliant."

And there it was, all laid out before her. The plan. How the world was held together. Glow-worms. Phosphorescence. They were the links. The staples that held the world together.

This was the city of fusion. André was full of shit.

Together, apart: life went on.

"Wilms. Look, maybe it's the drugs. But I understand. The city of fusion exists *anyway*. We don't have to create it. Fusion, fission—they're the same thing. All right, so they're not the same thing. They're exact opposites. But they can co-exist. Don't you see? I'm right to leave him. We've *got* to split up. It's fission. Right?"

Wilma hesitated before replying, looking at her friend, trying to remain on her feet in the increasingly lively swell.

"Yeah, right. Fission fuckin' chips, sweetheart."

And suddenly Lilith was off. Scampering through the shallows. She could only stand in one place for so long. Concentrate on one thing. She climbed back up the beach and swung across towards the bonfire. Everybody was bombed. Kelvin was the only one still on his feet, but he was swaying like a skyscraper in an earthquake. His eyes were open but he wasn't seeing anything, nothing on *this* planet. She brushed her hair out of her face and looked back down the beach beyond the fire. A ball of light was floating towards her, bobbing from left to right, getting steadily bigger. Then coming right at her over the fire, and among a terrifying clatter of sticks and shattering lights, Wilma, whose face had been the bobbing light, stopped abruptly in front of her—panting, sweating, her eyes like 8-balls.

"Wilms."

"What is it, kid?"

"Look at them."

This page: black short-sleeve stretch fabric shirt £39 by Jigsaw Menswear; black glazed cotton underpants £30 by Helmut Lang Underwear.

So what if you can't see them? Whole fucking point. Give them a picture taken at night without a flash, and with no fucking picture—but get the names in the captions. That's fashion photography in the 1990's. That's styling.

"Wilms."

Lilith danced around the fire, snapping the felled bodies of her friends of friends. She homed in on André, focused right through him so he was just a blur.

Opposite page: red viscose pointelle polo top and red wool/nylon mix gabardine reflective trousers both to order by John Bartlett. *This page:* black tie with stitch detail £65 by Paul Smith.

Snap snap.

Little flames licked around the soles of the Sue Engels shoes which had now almost completely melted away.

Snap snap snap.

"Wilms. Help me change the film. Help me change the fucking film."

"Lilith. Try not to throw *quite* so much sand in the camera. Lilith, what are you doing?"

Bending down over André's body. His eyes had rolled back. Hand held above his mouth. Feeling for a pulse.

Oh my sweet Christ.

He'd overdone it. Boy, had he overdone it.

Before she really knew what she was doing—snap.

It'll look good. No one will know.

Snap snap snap snap—snap snap snap.

Jonathon Staines

Carl's hands are thrumming the steering wheel, following the frenetic drumbeats of the jungle tape. I am on the back seat, wedged between Doughnut and Andy. It is 1am and, even for July, it is hot inside that old black Granada. Parked parallel to the river, the car is at the end of the Thames- where all its junk flows east into the sea. From the car's smoky windows I see the blinking seafront, its drunken casualties and shouting teenagers.

"Oi, Mark, d'ya want some o'this?" Andy clasps a can of lager in his gold- ringed fingers.

"Yeah, okay. Open the window, will ya?" I take a swig. Doughnut silently offers me the spliff he's just rolled meticulously and I swap it for the can.

"What're we gonna do then?" I ask, "We're not just gonna just sit 'ere all fuckin' night are we?" I hope they don't sense my desperation.

Not for the first time, Carl has been chucked out of Joe Friday's for dealing without the nod from the bouncers. At least they didn't take him out to the fire escape for a kicking. The bastards took his bag of pills and he is not happy.

Doughnut tries to lighten the atmosphere: "Right, listen, right, there's this geezer goes into a knockin' shop with two mates. There's three doors right— one's £10, one's £15 and one's £25..."

Without warning, Carl starts the engine and guns it before closing his eyes and gulping back some beer. He jerks us out of the carpark like he's watched too much Miami Vice.

"Shut up Doughnut. Just shut fuckin' up," he says solemnly.

"No, no 'ang on right..." Doughnut pleads, his face sweating as he puffs hastily on a fag. The car swings out onto the road. Carl turns up the music but Doughnut will not be drowned out.

"The geezer goes in the £10 door. Comes out 'alf hour la'er and 'is mates go, 'What was that like?' 'E goes, 'Fuckin' brilliant. She put a pineapple ring round me cock, put some whipped cream on it and ate it. Fantastic...'"

Andy is smiling and looking at me. I smile weakly then turn to look out of the window. Girls in short skirts and long boots walk arm in arm through empty drinks cans and chip papers scattered outside the video arcades. Andy, craning out of the window, yells: "You fuckin' slappers!"

I remember asking myself how I came to be in a car with these people—

how had the twists of my life led to this group, this car, this road? As far as I was concerned, we were just four kids who had no-one else to talk to in the lunch-break.

No different from the scores of other pale-faced no-hopes, we drifted around the streets in old Fords or Volkswagens, rather than try to engage with the town itself. You can be numb in a car, be nowhere in particular, be still even when you're moving. In the time it takes an image to move through your eyes and register, you are already somewhere else. In a car, it is always now. The windscreen is like a televsion, you can skim channels, fast forward, pause and record. You can shrink your shrivelled attention span as small as you like.

"…Geezer goes into the £15 room. Comes out 'alf hour la'er. Massive grin on his face. 'Is mates go, 'What 'appened?' 'E goes, 'The bird put a pineapple ring on me dick, whipped cream, anuvver pineapple ring, more cream and a cherry. Fa-an-tastic.'"

"Where we goin', Carl?" The joke is killing me.

"Dunno."

On the back of Carl's baseball cap I read: 'Chicago Bulls'. I wish he'd eject through the roof like a jettisoned pilot.

Instead, I try to sound helpful: "That caff's open 24 hours."

"Oh yeah." He takes the car over a railway bridge. I'm holding the spliff again and I toke. The tape finishes with a click and the seat softens under my head. Quietness has filled the car. The only discernible sound is the engine humming through the gears. Carl breaks the moment.

"I reckon I'm a prince in this town. People respect me. I've got mates. Loads o'mates. I can get birds. I do whatever I want."

Andy leans forward, gripping the passenger seat. "Oh yeah, tha's right, mate. It's like you've got everyfin' innit?"

"I ain't fuckin' finished my joke yet." Doughnut resumes the grim tale,

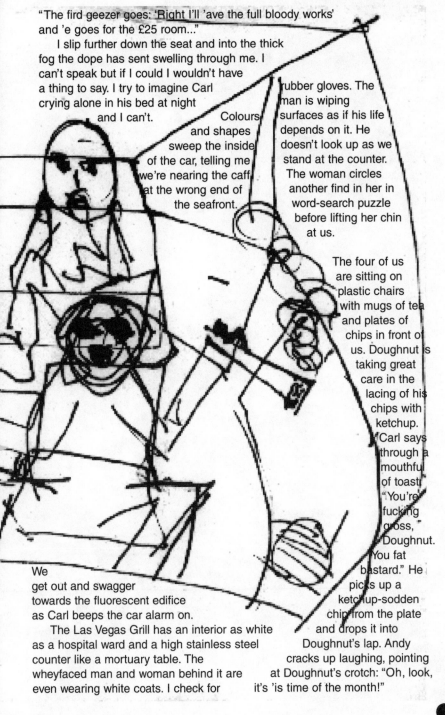

"The fird geezer goes: 'Right I'll 'ave the full bloody works' and 'e goes for the £25 room..."

I slip further down the seat and into the thick fog the dope has sent swelling through me. I can't speak but if I could I wouldn't have a thing to say. I try to imagine Carl crying alone in his bed at night and I can't. Colours and shapes sweep the inside of the car, telling me we're nearing the caff at the wrong end of the seafront.

rubber gloves. The man is wiping surfaces as if his life depends on it. He doesn't look up as we stand at the counter. The woman circles another find in her in word-search puzzle before lifting her chin at us.

The four of us are sitting on plastic chairs with mugs of tea and plates of chips in front of us. Doughnut is taking great care in the lacing of his chips with ketchup. Carl says through a mouthful of toast "You're fucking gross, Doughnut. You fat bastard." He picks up a ketchup-sodden chip from the plate and drops it into Doughnut's lap. Andy cracks up laughing, pointing at Doughnut's crotch: "Oh, look, it's 'is time of the month!"

We get out and swagger towards the fluorescent edifice as Carl beeps the car alarm on.

The Las Vegas Grill has an interior as white as a hospital ward and a high stainless steel counter like a mortuary table. The wheyfaced man and woman behind it are even wearing white coats. I check for

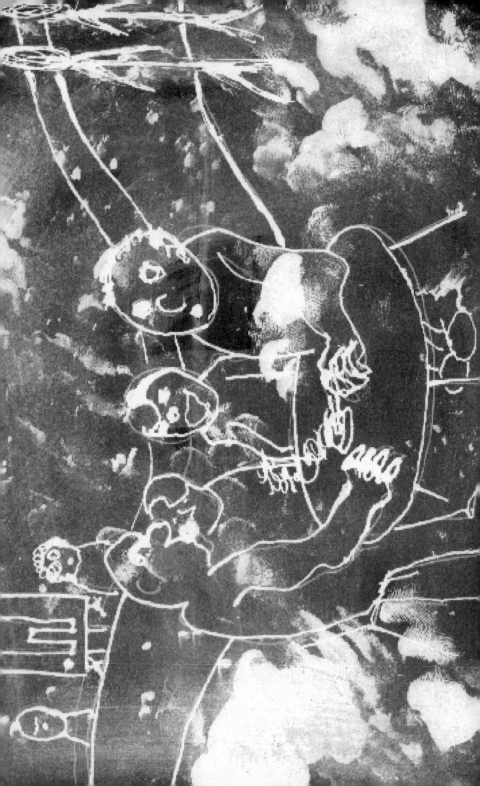

The man in the white coat looks nervous. He is oriental and in his fifties. Andy turns to him, grinning:

"Alight, Ping-Pong? Ah-So!"

"You're the arse'ole, Andy," I say, "Sit down and have another chip. It'll match the one on your shoulder."

"What you on about?"

"Forget it, just sit down and shut up." Luckily, he does.

Apart from the mad looking bloke by the window, we are alone until two young, smartly-dressed guys come in. As they come through the door, only I notice them. The others haven't seen, thank God.

Doughnut simultaneously finishes his chips and the joke started in the car:

"...and the bloke comes out and 'is mates go, '*Well?*' and he says, 'Brilliant! The bird put *three* pineapple rings on me dick, whipped cream, chocolate sauce, 'undreds and fowsands *and* a cherry.' 'Is mates go, 'Fuckin' ell, tha's amazing.' 'E goes, 'Yeah, it was so good, I *ate it myself!*'" Doughnut sits back with a look of post-coital satisfaction. Andy and Carl snigger half-heartedly. I drop three sugarlumps into my tea and stir for what seems like an hour. Doughnut is launching into a joke about 'queers'. I look at the oriental man and the crazy bloke by the window and hope neither of them understands a word of it.

Andy is listening to Doughnut like a man at church. Through the wisps of his cigarette smoke, his eyes are narrowed. Tiny reflections of the cafe's strip lighting make his eyes alive with light. I look down past his Reebok sweatshirt to the gold and onyx rings on his fingers and between them, the Superking with its sausage of sagging ash. Suddenly he lolls back, shuddering with laughter and the ash scatters across the table.

The word-search woman shuffles straight over and starts lifting plates and ashtrays so she can wipe under them. Her hair is dyed the colour of aubergines and, as she wipes, charms on her bracelet rattle. Lost somewhere between forty and fifty, she has the sour look of someone cheated. Andy pounces.

"Oh, tha's it love, you're good at that. Scrubbing. You're a lovely scrubber. What you doin' after? I like a woman in uniform y'know. 'Ow's about you n' me out the back la'er on, eh? That'll cheer you up wun it?...eh?" Now Doughnut and Carl are the captive, pliant audience. "Actually, actually, I like the more mature woman. I do, dun I Carl? You ask Carl. I love 'em. Varicose veins are my favourite...Ya know why? Cos they remind me of me mum..." By this point, Carl and Doughnut are hysterical. The woman stops wiping the table and fixes Andy with an impassive stare.

"If I'd been your mother, darlin', I'd've throttled you at birth." She retreats to the counter. Carl and Doughnut sing in unison: "Wow!" Andy is silent.

The two smart men scrape their chairs back and finish their teas standing. They slide back into their leather jackets as they walk to the till.

"Everything alright for you my loves?" The woman's smile reveals bad teeth. One of the men hands her a fiver.

"Yes, fine thanks, Sylvia. The drinks were fine. It's just a bit noisy in here tonight. See you next week." The woman hands him the change.

"Yeah, see ya darlin'. Take care o'yourselves."

Andy mutters loudly: "Fuckin' ponces... they sound like a right couple of arse-bandits." He shouts after them, doing his best to sound condescending: "We're only tryin' to 'ave a laugh. Y'know, a bit of a giggle." He looks at Doughnut, Carl and me. "God, I fuckin' can't stand queers. I don't know 'ow they fuckin' get like it—ya know what I mean?"

Carl and Doughnut both say "Yeah."

I stir my tea again but there's not much left to stir.

Fifteen minutes later, we're in the car again. Carl calls it cruising. Other cars pass us, all blacked out windows and thumping bass. Sometimes, the windows are wound down and an occupant in a back-to-front baseball cap leans out and yells: "*Wa-hey!*" or "You wankers!" Carl, Andy and Doughnut are not angered. To them, this is a greeting, a signal of respect. "Fuck off you flash cunts!" they yell back happily. I just want to put my key in the front door and my head on a pillow. I take Doughnut's spliff in search of sweet dissolution.

"Cocksuckers! Faggots!" Carl has his window down, and his tone is not jovial. "Andy, there's them two poofs. From the caff." Andy leans out too.

"Goin' 'ome for a shag, girls?"

Silently, one of the men raises two fingers and my stomach turns. This is just what Carl was waiting for. He brings the car to a slow stop at the kerb and leaves the engine running.

"Carl—" I begin, but it's too late. He, Andy and Doughnut are out of the car, loping over to the two men, whose smart dress now seems like a thrown gauntlet. My heart is pounding. I hurry from the back of the car towards the scene. I can't speak. The men do not run. They remain where they are, arms at their sides, facing their three aggressors.

"What do you want?" one of them says.

"You two are fuckin' queers unt ya?" Carl asks.

The taller of the two men smiles and then laughs.

"No. Whatever gave you that idea?"

"Yes, you are," says Carl, "I just know. I can tell. You look like poofs. You sound like it. And you smell like queers. So don't give it that." He makes a gabbing mouth movement with his hand.

"Well, I'm not. Are you queer Stephen?" The blond man asks his friend.

"Not as far I know."

"Bullshit," Carl is belligerent. "Anyway, you was rude to us in the caff."

"Oh, this is absurd," the shorter man says nervously.

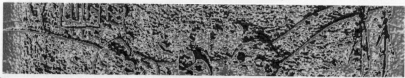

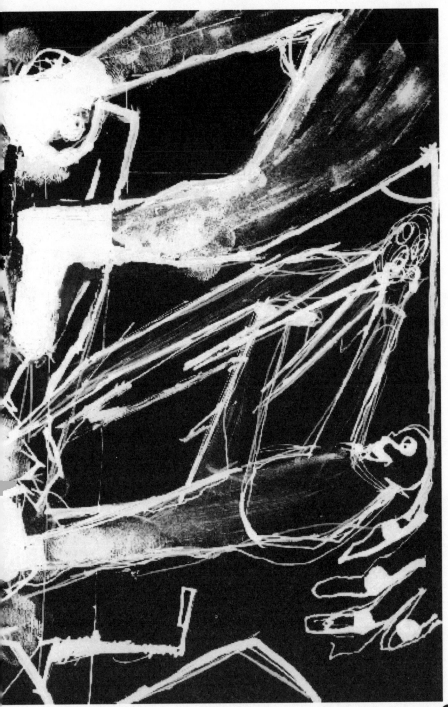

"I'll show you what's fuckin' absurd!" Carl head-butts the man with the appalling sound and movement of a cracking whip. The man staggers back, yelling, holding his furiously bleeding nose. Andy shoots two punches at the other man's face and he is down. Doughnut is busy finishing the job, kicking both in the stomach, ribs and groin.

I am trying not to be sick. Hands on my head, I'm shouting like a lunatic:

"Oh Jesus! Jesus Christ! Carl! What are you fucking doing, you dickheads? Just stop…*Stop it!*"

Already they're on their way back to the Granada, silent and business-like. Andy turns to face me.

"Shut the fuck up, Mark. What's wrong with you? For fuck's sake shut your mouth and get in the car now, before someone sees and calls the Old Bill."

Rooted to the spot, I look round at the two casualties on the pavement. They are moving only slightly. One of them is sobbing. In the orange haze of the streetlamp, the blood on their hands and faces is as black as oil. Doughnut hastily pisses into someone's front garden. The acrid stench fills my nostrils.

"I'll stay here. I'll walk home."

"Don't be a prat. D'ya wanna get done or something?"

"I haven't done anything, Andy. I'm not the one with blood on my hands."

"You fuckin' are now." I see the motion of his arm but I don't move.

It's like I need to feel the collision of his hate-filled fist with my face. I'm stumbling like a drunk. My head is spinning. When I stop puking, I wipe the mixture of blood and vomit from my mouth. I go over to the two men.

"Erm...are you..okay?"

"Fuck off!" the big one croaks, "Does it look like it?…Anyway, why aren't you with your *friends*?"

"They're not my friends."

"Who are they then?"

"I dunno," I answer. An uneasy silence follows. Eventually he says, "You look like shit."

"Thanks. How's your mate?" He gently shakes the other man.

"Stephen?…Stephen?" Stephen groans and mumbles, "Leave me alone…"

I step over him, heading for the phone box on the corner of the street.

"Where you going?" Stephen's friend asks.

"Dial 999."

"For an ambulance?"

"Nope. The police. Then an ambulance."

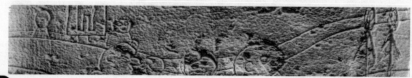

MAAA GICK, MOMENTS

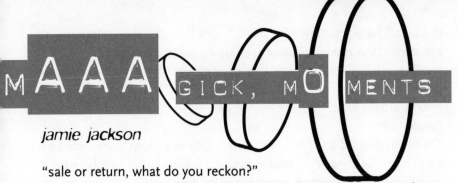

jamie jackson

"sale or return, what do you reckon?"

"dunno. I've tried it before and never made any money, you know what I mean?"

"fair enough like, but just bring us back the pills you don't sell."

it was certainly a tempting offer, Jarvis thought, looking round the cold flat he was renting off a local smack head who hated him anyway.

"listen, there's Teddy'n'that, he'll watch your back when you're in there." Chinny got out a bank bag and handed it to Jarvis. "I'll give you fifteen for starters, good uns as well, doves, and whatever you can't sell bring back."

"right, okay... so if I don't sell any I can bring'em all back yeah?"

"fuucking too right, don't worry about it. we lay 'em on for a tenner, you can sell 'em for fifteen, that's a fiver each time."

we lay 'em on for a tenner, you can sell 'em for fifteen, that's a fiver each time

Jarvis had a good look at Chinny. he'd always liked him, looked up to him...a drug dealer with a conscience, a kinda Northern town guru for all the upcoming lads...what a scheme, all sponsored by Thatcher as well, you know, get your dole, invest in an ounce, sell it, build up your float and most vitally your contacts, and when the right business opportunity comes up, you're the one to feel the benefit of the local expansion. beautiful, Capitalism at its most virile and beneficial.

"okay then Chinny, nice one, cheers. when d'you want me to come round then with the money for 'em?"

"sunday night. around seven'll be alright, me Gran'll be at bingo by then you see." Chinny laughed, "its good to hear you subscribing to the school of positive thinking, focussing on the money instead of the pills." he passed him the joint. "right I'm off," then, stopping at the door, "how much is Coconut charging you for this gaff?"

"well nothing apart from the money for the bills, you know gas'n'that"

"that's alright innit?"

"yeah."

Chinny fucked off and Jarvis sat on the sofa in a room surrounded by someone else's posters, books, photos, feeling like a burglar who'd never got out, and looked at the E's in the bag.

fuck me, he thought, a few months ago these babies would'a been Chrimbo. fuck Quality Street, I'd be having me own magic moments.

the place was jumping when he got there. to him it was still a new concept, the old Carlton crooners club turned into a topspot for ravers, with coachloads balling their way in from wrist-slashing gaffs like Barrow and Preston. he'd only been back from abroad a couple of months and had missed this metamorphosis. when he'd left this had been a graveyard of northern soul burnouts and cabaret beerguts giving cheap thrills to all the old fuckers from Morecambe.

"can of Red Stripe please."

clutching the classic mother's breast, he took a suckle and started on a wander round.

where the fuck do I start? look at 'em all, some of these fuckers were in the choir when I was at school, now look at 'em, tops off, chins jutted out like Jimmy Hill's cousins, sweating their arses off, they look like they're sorted already.

he got at the back of the scrum of people by the wall and had a scan round. he saw Ted and gave him the nod. it was alright for him, every fucker knew him, was scared of him, felt like it was a privilege to buy off him and line his pockets. still, at least he's on my side and if he's not bothered about me treading on his toes, then maybe this'll be a goer after all; come on then lets do it to the crowd. he took a dive right into the ruck of civilisation letting their hair down and zoomed in on some lasses.

"want any E's? come on, they're good for you...no?...come on, you know it makes sense in your heart of hearts, come on be straight with yourself, let it go, fuck your parents off, they're not you, you're here, this is your time, take it while you can before marriage has you. no?...they're good for you, especially if you're dyslexic, you know a letter you *can* rely on, get it??? come on, don't fail me I'm giving you my best cheesy grin, can't you see? fuck me, I'm not selling poison y'know!!"

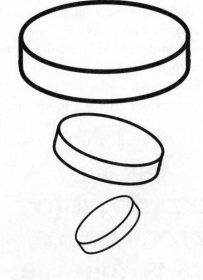

"we've just taken two, so we don't need 'em."

"oh,...right, but what about next wee-"

"no ta, good try though. better patter."

"fancy a shag?"

yeah, this isn't too bad, open your mouth, let the shit roll out, have a crack with Joe Public and get your wares peddled. it's got to beat being a cog in the wheel of industry, with all those whistles creasing their faces.

taking a look around, he saw the mirrors on the wall and the tunnel that led down to the girls bogs. a home from home. a natural habitat. he could bring out the maternal in them. hey, I'm a reconstructed lad, can't you tell?

"yeah alright mate. E's? good old fashioned E's, no additives and certainly no preservatives. want any?"

"nah thanks. but me mate might."

fucking yes, let's have you, I feel like getting her name and recording it for when I get on 'This is Your Life'. yes Aspel, this is the one, she didn't want one herself, but her fucking mate did.

she brought the bloke over. "how many d'you want?"

"just the one...actually, what have you got?"

o-oh, a pretension merchant, you want to get yourself to the university..."actually they're doves, fresh off the press from the Dam."

a blank stare.

"Amsterdam."

"oh," the punter's visage broke into a relieved smile, like he'd just found out he had a kid, but it wasn't his sister he'd fertilised.

"okay then, how much?"

for a moment it looked like maybe it was his mother he'd impregnated.

"fifteen quid."

"oh nice one." he got in his pockets and right to the meat of the deal.

"here."

oh those notes are crisp, pass'em into the jacket, get the pills out and let's get cooking. one down, fourteen to go...

Jarvis took his beer off the ledge and over its rim saw a lad in blazer and tie, totally in the wrong gaff, bear down on him.

"hey, you remember me don't you?" he allowed this to sink in. "cubs, we used to go..."

"no sorry mate." fucking hell I do remember this plum, had a bit of a thing going with the Akela, got caught with his woggle in a compromising position. "tell you what, d'you want any E's ?",

"ah? oh, well, not really, I'm not into pharmaceuticals."

"right, see ya."

by now though, he couldn't go wrong, the place was rammed with willing punters, happy to boost his benevolence fund for the next morning's shop down at Joseph's, the local supplier of top notch

I feel like recording it for when I get on 'This is Your Life'. yes Aspel, this is the one clobber. sure it was inverted snobbery, buying all the labels that hopefully no-one else could afford, but life had to be for something, and burning two hundred quid on a jacket seemed as good a pastime as any.

"HOY! YEAH YOU. WHAT THE FUCK ARE YOU DOING?"

Jarvis looked up at the lad who now grabbed his jacket and squinted through little round glasses.

"what you on about?"

"shut the fuck up, just shut the fuck up. what've you got in your pocket? a fuckin' bag of pills?"

"ay?...yeah...why?" said Jarvis slowly, looking right in the geezer's eyes. he saw power. just pure power and evil.

shit, what the fucking hell's going on with this pitbull? where's Ted at when I need him?

"you've been serving those up haven't you? right, with me right now, come on."

"but, Ted, he'll-"

"SHUT IT! come on. the bogs. let's get to the fucking bogs and sort this shit out."

Christ that's quite a good example of gallows humour, Jarvis couldn't help reflecting, as he was shunted through the dripping, sodden meat that danced away.

"right in here." he slammed Jarvis through the cubicle door and had him up against the wall. "right give us your money."

"you what, I haven't got any, I... I've only sold one."

"look," he pulled out a shooter from his jacket and dug it in his stomach. "give us the money and the pills."

"yeah alright." he brought out the bag, "Jesus, don't shoot me please. here."

the bloke blinked through his glasses, with what looked like a smile.

"oh don't worry, I'm not going to shoot you, whatever gave you that idea." with that he backed out of the cubicle and stood panting for a second. then he ripped off his bomber jacket, and then his shirt, grinning as the buttons all pinged off.

"what the fuck?..."

"no sir in fact far from shoot you I'm going to," he was now down to a string vest, which showed up a full thatch of matted carpet hair, "I'm going to serenade you. I do hope you appreciate it, penned from my own fair hand:

"maaa gick, mO ments,   when two worlds collide
maaa gick, mO ments,   when we slip and slide
maaa gick, mO ments,   get a load of this
maaa gick, mO ments,   you've just had the piss...taken."

"what d'you reckon?"
before he could answer, Chinny burst through the door and flash!!! took a snap of the happy couple, one with a rose between his teeth, one without. He flashed him a grin, "welcome to the crew mate, welcome to the crew."

apocalypse
now and then

duncan brown

It had been fully thirty years since his very best music and Luke could hardly say that he hadn't been warned.

"Don't go," they'd all told him, "Get a bottle of vino in and stack up the best of 'em, 'Fire Magic', 'Dark Alchemy', 'Sacred and Profane'...don't go see what's left of him now. Once you lose that perfect picture, you'll never get him back."

Mary saw the problem in different terms: "Do you really play this for enjoyment? It sounds like a gaggle of teenage girls all screaming and squealing at once."

"My point exactly," he'd replied, without really getting it till much later.

They might have swung him too, had Luke not bought his ticket weeks before, the very day he'd heard about the gig. Fifteen quid a shot those tickets. No mean investment by anyone's standards, but little short of irresponsible by his own.

Nothing could now
persuade him to
stay home, not even
the thought of
filming another
night of riots from
the top of the
flats, or following
it on the Internet,
depending on where
it kicked off.

They'd pretty much had ringside seats most of yesterday, but the action could shift so quickly, you had to keep online in case it skipped a dozen blocks out of view, up to the prison or down to the barracks and the roadblocks.

Besides, Luke wasn't sure he bought this routine about the old man being past it. So, the guy hadn't played Europe in over two decades—he wasn't ready to bury him in a boxed set just yet. Live was where free jazz came into its own: for weeks now Luke had been anticipating getting right in up close to his all-time favourite improviser, close enough to smell the sweat, to see the rope of spit stringing off the mouthpiece, the furnace of passion in the eyes. Let them wheel him on in a bed or a chair if they had to; Luke couldn't care if he was hunched up double, playing the bloody sax through a hole in his neck. He knew a true and honest note when he heard one and that had fuck all to do with perfect pitch.

It wasn't so easy to explain. Half the time he didn't bother, but when he did, Luke invoked all the usual suspects in his attempt to define the music's potency. The trouble was, nobody believed in culture anymore, not in that way. The mechanics of media, now that was something else, but culture as a political force?

"I'm telling you! It played a part. It made a bloody difference."

"For fuck's sake, Luke, it's only music after all. It's hardly gonna help when the shit hits the fan."

"Look, don't blame me for your cynicism. What's that old line about dancing and architecture? Well this is like comparing...oh I don't know... writing formal business letters and action painting in blood, your **own** sweat and blood."

Later his rant reverbed round his head and he despaired of doing the music justice.

It was always the same: grasping for the perfect analogy and coming away with something trite and empty. If the musicians could have said it with words, maybe they'd have done so. Instead they'd extemporised sound, from the spidery, arhythmic and fragile to the liberating rage of brute force. Luke's mistake was to try and define it, when the very point was that it aimed at a place beyond words.

And what did it matter in the end? His had never been a mainstream music, too threatening, too alienating. If time had changed the saxman and he'd mellowed with age, then Luke for one was ready to cut him some slack.

You'd think you'd get a view of the stage at that price, but the diners got preference and you had to squint past bowls of glutinous pasta and greasy garlic bread. With the huge video screen behind the drum kit and the series of monitors, the room was like a brightly lit canteen-cum-conference room.

Rushed off her feet, a raven-haired waitress turned with a tray of empties to catch Luke milking a snifter from his hip-flask. A pound coin shrugged its way into her jar, not as a bribe, but because he knew the workers depended on tips. They certainly weren't in on the door heist. Two minutes later she was back, tip-toeing through the tables to deliver piss-coloured lagers stuffed with limes to a suited group who sat there cracking lewd comments about her arse. With a pragmatic smile, she tucked their handful of silver in her pocket and turned to pluck a fresh glass from her tray, which she slid toward Luke with a wink and was gone.

Sitting back, he wondered which should have been the better reason to stay home—the fact that time takes away, or that the place was stuffed to the shirts with people like this. He wanted to focus on the music, but, with everything that was going down on the streets just now, he felt like he'd turned his back on something and crossed some unspeakable line. He wanted to slip backstage and find him, apologise for paying twelve quid to come and see him here, in this place.

Luke entertained a brief fantasy about smuggling him out the back and taking him to the pub gig around the corner.

He could make some calls, get a few real people down to swell out the crowd. But of course, he was forgetting the money.

That was four musicians on the road for starters and these guys had paid their dues, you understand. They had to be fed, clothed, sheltered and watered. Likely as not, they'd have families to support. No wonder that they had to play here, in this white collar restaurant, this antiseptic lah-di-dah canteen.

Besides, he was forgetting that whatever the weathermen might have said, tonight of all nights, no-one could be relied on for anything. He was still thinking yesterday's logic, yesterday's travelzones. Even as he sat there, sinking in his seat and waiting for showtime, he knew things were shifting back at street level. He should have been out there, doing his bit. It was as if he had a phantom limb, a nervous third arm that itched and twitched beneath the table. A molotov arm, for those missions improbable, if and when.... Well, he would only have to get it right the once—one well-timed, well-primed ambush, a quick burst of power in just the right place.

Luke had his laptop with him and would have liked to whip it out there and then, to check how things were shaping up. But there was nothing like a crowd like this to resurrect the old Luddite in him. Some part of him yearned for poetry over binary and he had always felt that however you chose to subvert it, you were still playing their games on their own home turf. He dabbled here and there as it suited, but always with a nag of resistance. Probably too self-conscious. Well, if you saw someone hacking at a keyboard in some swanky place like this, you would just know straight out what they were up to. What else was left? Just blood money deals, here at home or Interstate—the same old Same Old.

The stage introductions came treacle-swamped and overdone—this skinny little thing jumping about all hipspeak and swagger and imagined Noo Yawk accent. God, she made Luke's ranting monologues sound like considered academic essays. Maybe it embarrassed the band, because they shambled onstage while she was still whipping up the hype, causing her to be drowned beneath a swelling wave of clapping and cheering, wolf whistles and hollering. Even Luke got caught up in the circus, forgetting where he was, flushing hot and deliriously expectant. By the end of the first solo, his childlike grin had been kicked in the teeth. He'd expected a certain mellowing, some lapses into straightish blues and even ballads, but not this, surely **anything** but this, this horrible syrupy mess, this... nightmare slop of fusion, for Christ's sake! Fusion was no good to anyone. **Fission** on the other hand—now **that** would be a music!

Atomic, destructive, energy music. Molecular music, to split worlds in two.

He kept telling himself it would change, it could only get better, but the entire first set floundered in the same turgid stodge. Where was the passion, the fire, the anger? The hardware of the drum kit dominated more than just his view, the very sound of the music itself, clumsily rooting it to earth. He wanted to leave just ten minutes in, but the cost of the ticket and the told-you-so's back home made him sit it out in the hope of one moment of magic. His head was in his hands at the end of the set, when the waitress came tapping at his shoulder.

"Hey, pesado. Why you look so sad? You want maybe come something smoke?" She tugged impatiently at his sleeve as he bent to gather his coat and battered case.

"Venga. Come quick. Only ten minutes."

She led him off round the dogleg of the bar, past the side of the stage and through a little door marked staff only. They were in a corridor backstage. Luke could see the rest of the band through the open door of the dressing room, but his one-time main man was nowhere to be seen.

"Quick, we go here—secret smoke." She pushed him through another door into a dark cupboard of a room, a musty, poky annex to the dressing room next door. "We smoke here, very quick, *puff puff*, we go again. Very nice secret smoke. Manager still happy, still stupid... We *very* happy! Okay? Good."

Luke sensed her very close in the darkness and heard the rustle as she stooped to pull a joint from some hiding place near her boot.

"Why you sad? Music is too safe, much too easy, no?" It was only as the match flared that they saw the saxman in the corner.

"La puta madre! Perdona, perdona. Normalmente, here no is dressing room. Perdona, señor! We go now, we go."

A compact sketch of a smile eased onto his face as he held up his hand, open-palmed in command, before sweeping it across the chairs in invitation.

"You been working the bar? Figure you deserve a little smoke." His hand spun a little spiral in the air, encouraging them to sit and be his guests. The waitress sparked the joint and offered it to their host, but he closed his palm against his chest,

"Time was... but my lungs got other ideas."

Luke was won over instantly. Now he could see him up close, face-to-face, he felt guilty for condemning the playing. His clothes still bore some reference to the infamous extravagance of the old days. The purple of his sharply tailored trousers was just two shades removed from the unfathomable rubied black of his face and he had a matching waistcoat and a long dark cloak to top it off. Still, it was hard to equate this laconic, disarmingly graceful man with the old stories of a shamanistic warrior. You had to try and divorce the myths and ancient history from the twists and tiny tragedies of life. From the state of his skin and the slight tremor in his hands, Luke guessed that the rumours of old addictions through the fallow years had not been whipped up from thin air. Yet despite the physical ravages, he still radiated strength and self-possession from some firmly anchored core. The waitress went back to work, but her earlier question lingered in the room, with question marks, Spanish style, at either end of the sentence. He must have heard every scathing word, but was either indifferent or too polite to bring it up.

"Say, what's in the bag?"

Luke flipped the catches and showed him the machine, "It's a laptop computer."

"That much I can see. You blowing up aliens while we playing, or checking the overnight markets?"

"What? No look, I don't normally cart it around, but what with the riots... or maybe you haven't heard?" And then Luke was off and running, telling about the riots and all that had lead to them: the end of public housing; Securicorps, the private sector law enforcers sent in to rout the police strike; the bloody assaults on fortified squats; the arrests, the beatings, the body bags. The call went up for the second set, but the musician simply bolted the door, insisting on more details, making comparisons, demanding more evidence. Luke said nothing more, but flicked on the computer, doubleclicked the page and let the portamodem and the rooftop website editors do the rest.

The old man watched in silence, but some spark gave him away, something buried deep beyond his eyes. It wasn't until the management was hammering and shouting at the door that he finally drew breath to speak.

"This thing got an output? Can you send the visuals to a monitor?"

"Sure you can, the lead's tucked in the back. Two-way sends. Just hook up the ports and you're away."

"Listen. I'm due back on, there's no time to explain. Is it cool with you if I just borrow this awhile?"

For the first 10 minutes, he just stood solo on the stage, back to the audience, cape rippling slightly as his body gently swayed to music in his head. The saxophone hung loose at his side as he watched events unfold on the screen. All around the room, monitors relayed the same jerky pictures. Wave after wave of baton charging cops in riot gear; armoured vehicles and military police; blackshirted Securicorps; CS gas, smoke and water canon; defiant youths with handkerchief masks, streaming with tears; skulls cracked, caked and oozing blood; young parents running blind, or cowering in alleyways, dirt-smeared kids clutched to their chests. At first the audience didn't notice, but five minutes in the freshly earplugged sound technician started to mix computer audio through the desk, barely audible at first, but gradually tweaking it over the clink of champagne and cocktails. One by one they fell silent, laughter and chatter giving way to the inescapable cacophony of sirens, roars and screams—gunfire, explosions and the dull percussive thuds of flying brickwork and heads against tarmac.

Was that a saxophone now, or a siren? The instrument was poised at his lips, but it was hard to tell at first. Little by little the horn imposed its signature—long, deep, tortured laments, peppered with lightning fast clusters at the top of the register. Slowly but surely it gathered pace: ever-increasing bursts of violence, shrill harmonics, guttural honks, drones, dirges and discordant overtones. There was a reference to an old tune, 'Dark Alchemy', barely recognisable in this setting. The playing was living off its own energies now, self-fulfilling, recycling like a virus, feeding back on itself and spewing out redoubled. Now it was a barrage—deafening, fundamental, unrelenting. Luke was humbled by this noise of nothing on earth. Way beyond circular breathing; it was as if superhuman energies were feeding air through the saxophonist's lungs, as if nature and magic, the very forces of creation were at hand, huffing and puffing their apocalyptic blast. Inside the venue, glasses, lamps and windows imploded as the pinstripe and fur fought to escape from the din.

Blood poured from ears and noses, sheer terror distorting blanched faces as they ran from their shattered reflections.

Infernally loud, the sound attacked at all extremes, the bass churning in hyperventilation and the top end slicing up into ear piercing vertigo, oscillating round the frequencies of brainwaves, heartbeat and bowels. Luke just stood there, laughing by the speakers, embracing the chaos and baptised in the mounting tide of mortal funk. It could have been delirium, his own sweet, stupid madness, but in the minute or two before blacking out, he could have sworn that the polarities had been reversed: the music no longer took its cue from the screen—instead the pictures were driven by the music. As time itself disrupted, the panic fanfare seemed to rent the horizon. The air echoed with the scream of unseen energies. Helmets flew from the heads of policemen and soldiers. Armoured vehicles skidded, screeched and overturned, combusting instantaneously. Sheet glass and roof tiles leapt from nearby buildings, split in jagged fragments and rained down on troops already fleeing their posts at barricades and checkpoints. Armed with sticks and stones and whatever lay to hand, the crowds turned and stood their ground in a clatter of unruly percussion.

CAROL SWAIN
SOFT CONCRETE

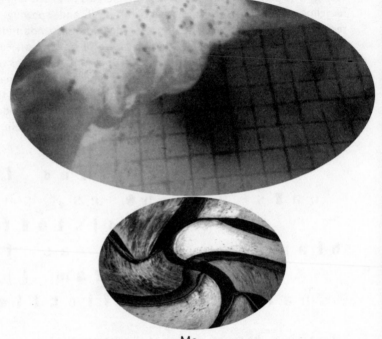

Me
and Ade spent a lot of our
time down the back alleys. Always,
always when the drains were being dug and
then covered over, he couldn't resist, you'd step
down there and see it: ADRIAN cut into the wet concrete
and his weird fucking messages—JESUS SAYS READ MORE
MEAT, MY FACE IS BETTER THAN YOUR FACE, MUM BUY US
A DOG. Sometimes he'd date them, '86, '87, '89. '88 was missed
'cos that's the year his dad died.

I remember, shit it was horrible. He (Ade's dad) would lie on the sitting room sofa with the curtains drawn, curled up like a kid, but moaning. I didn't know what he was up to then, but now I know it was dying. Slowly. He would drink that disgusting yellow Advocat stuff. It was the only thing he could keep down. He was eating himself up. Ade wouldn't talk about it. Something was eating his dad from the inside, an ulcer or tumour or something, anyway in a year his dad was dead.

So   it
was just Ade and his mum.

*   *   *   *   *   *   *   *

Ade changed. I didn't notice really at the time. Forget concrete. He started putting his mark on bigger things, what's the phrase—going off the rails. He went right off them. His mother didn't help. I didn't like her then; I don't now. She was busy running her craft shop. Selling shit to tourists, little Welsh dolls, toffee in tins with Snowdon on top, slate clocks. Who needs that stuff? Who needs it? Isn't it enough to see the fucking mountains and lakes and stuff, do you need to buy a tin of toffee? I mean how does toffee remind you of a fucking mountain? I don't know, I really don't.

Ade sort of got quieter but more violent. All of us were a bit wild looking back on it. Magic mushrooms, cider and Vodka mixed, dope, speed, smack even. Stuff off the hippies, all home grown.

Ade drank more. You'd have to pull the fucking bottle off his lips and SSSSSUUUUCCCCKKKK to get a drop.

He—all of us—would lie on the square around the war memorial like corpses. It embarrassed Ade's mother, my parents too. We were supposed to show some respect or something.

I could never do it but Ade took to stealing cars. He'd come round my yard with that look he always had when he'd got a car parked down a track. Sort of an 'are-you-coming-out-to-play-Gary?' look. We were fourteen, we didn't bloody play.

Anyway he'd always steal off people who he knew wouldn't drop him in it with the pigs if we got stopped, does that make sense? I mean like the drug dealing hippies for example, they'd never call the cops; the hippies had crap cars, mind.

We'd all get in the car, as many of the gang that could cram in there. Ade would drive, seeing as he stole it. Christ he was fast. Up the blind lanes – Bachie Road, over the top down by Coed Llan. No lights, never lights. Night.
"I'll see them coming by their lights," he'd say. "If ours are on I can't see what's coming."

Yeah.

We'd end up through a hedge or something and have to walk miles back, picking glass our of our hair.

We never hit nothing oncoming though, we were lucky.

Police gave us full-time hassle after a while. Just out walking they'd buzz us—"Poaching or picking?" they'd ask. Magic mushrooms they meant or fishing without permission. They'd always have a go at Ade 'cos he was mouthy with them.

"Everything in town belongs to everyone," he said, so he'd take anything that wasn't nailed down. If it was nailed down he'd come back later with a hammer.

When I say he was mouthy with the cops I don't mean like he shouted at them, no, he'd say funny things—"Are you happy?—REALLY HAPPY? Ask yourselves," he said to them once.

*   *   *   *   *   *

Yeah so he started to take anything he wanted, food, bikes, stupid books from the post office. Guide books—'Montgomeryshire for walkers'. He lived there; what use is Montgomeryshire for fucking walkers if you live there?

His mother had enough of him, kicked him out, so he went up the lake to live with some hippies, but he was in town all the time still.

One time he broke into the chemist shop, God we had a weekend, taking all this stuff, half of it we didn't know what it was or what it'd do to us. Pills, capsules we emptied the powder out of, syrup stuff, little glass things with liquid in, injection bottles.

I just puked. Total blackout.

"I could've cured myself of something by accident," Ade said.

He seemed to have more tolerance than anyone. He just sort of slumped in a corner of the long-hairs house and blinked once every two hours, smiling. He said after, he didn't know he was smiling, it must have been a muscle spasm. The next morning he cut himself, he said, and his blood was thick and black like treacle. I believed him, but I said never again.

Ade told us that some of the pills were this painkiller his dad used to take, Diamorphine I think.

"Good stuff," he said. I noticed he didn't share that around.

"Dead strong," he said. "Too much for you."

* * * * * *

I suppose I was thinking about him 'cos they're laying cable all over town now. Trenches everywhere. For cable TV.

Ade didn't like TV. The hippies weaned him off it he told us. He'd still be coming up to my place and we'd be watching and he'd be bored, standing by the window. Like the farm dogs when they get shut in.

Ade liked to be doing things. I'm not saying he was stupid 'cos he wasn't. No fucking way. He was useless in school mind, not that he was there much. The head wouldn't let him on the grounds till he cut his hair. He never cut it.

I know he wasn't stupid. He couldn't remember dates and stuff. The shit

they mark you on, History, Geography, Biology, but he knew things, like what people do to each other, I'm not talking about sex and all that. He'd be sitting drinking with us, and we'd be talking about someone's stupid parents, talking like, I don't know, fifteen year olds. But Ade would say something that would stop us, make us listen a bit. I can't remember—oh yeah, Dale's dad used to hit Dale a lot till Dale got too big, you know, big enough to hit back... "When I get older I'm going to kill him," Dale said. And Ade told him "No you won't. You'll just feel bad for him and kill your own kid."

I remember that. He didn't say 'kids', he said 'kid'. Only kid, like Ade.

*   *   *   *   *

Yeah, the cable laying, they're concreting over the paths. Some kid's already got in there, prime spot, boring— DARREN WAS HERE. Darren, mate, we fucking know where you are.

A cat has walked across too, and beside the pawprints someone else has written: SORRY. I thought of Ade. Straight away. I mean I know it couldn't have been him, but I could see him doing that. It would be the sort of shit he'd write.

Jay Welch — M O A

Lianne doesn't want to scream but she can't help it. Then she's angry at herself. Clumsy cow, what a stupid thing to do, really fucking stupid. She holds her wrist under the cold tap; a boiled pink patch appears on her white skin like the outline of a polaroid. She listens out anxiously, but all she can hear is the telly muttering away in the

it is, probably—he can't get comfy. Derek promised weeks ago that he'd get them a new bed, a kids' bed for Kurt. A mattress would be enough. She knows she'll have to have a go at him about it because Derek doesn't really know what it's like, having to make do.

Lianne turns off the tap and it takes a second or two before the

other room, and the quiet shshshsh of steam from the kettle. At least she didn't wake Kurt.

He was sound asleep ten minutes ago, so chances are he'll keep on through the night, fingers crossed. She wonders what it is he dreams about. Some mornings she wakes up and looks across to his cot, and he's screwed his blankets into a ball and twisted his arms and legs into awkward knots and his head's down the end where his feet ought to be, and one little fist will be crammed in his mouth to stop it up. He's too big for that cot now, even with the sides down: that's all

pain comes back to her wrist. Stupid how such a small thing could hurt so much.

In the bedroom Kurt stuffs his mouth with as many fingers as he can fit in it. The semi-darkness is full of monstrous things that he doesn't dare think about; when he heard that noise just now, they woke up and started shifting around. He shuts his eyes tight and wishes.

"Why did you have to go and do

that to yourself?" Derek says, aggrieved. "You want to take that off if it's a burn. Burns need to get the air."

"It looks horrible," Lianne argues. "It can't be worse than that bandage. Who ever heard of a glamour girl with a bloody great bandage round her arm?"

"I haven't said I'll do it."

"It's a job."

"He said he'd get you a job, Lianne," chips in Melanie. "Ungrateful cow." Lianne glares at her kid sister. Melanie stares back with the trace of a smirk. Kurt makes a grab for the ashtray.

"Girls, girls," says Derek, as Lianne lifts Kurt out of harm's way and joggles him on her knee. "Of course Lianne is grateful and she's going to give this job her all. Mr Harkness was most impressed by Lianne's audition. He told me, in confidence, mind,"—Derek taps his nose—"that it's been a long time since he's seen a girl like Lianne."

Lianne hugs her son; she can't help blushing a bit. Kurt wriggles, squealing impatiently. What he really wants is to get at Derek's fag butts and chew out those spongy bits that taste of smoke and mint.

Melanie plops heavily down onto the sofa. "Speck you'll want me to babysit, then? I could come round after school on Tuesday. If there's any money."

"I haven't said I'll do it yet," says Lianne, a bit less definite than before.

Terry Harkness pats his troubled belly and pours himself a brandy Alexander. He leans across the bar. "How old did you say she was?"

"Nineteen," Derek says.

"You sure about that, Del?"

Derek looks at him. It's a look that could mean a number of ings.

"Well," says Terry. "Keeps the punters happy, anyways."

Derek looks round the room. It's early yet and not many of the tables are occupied, but none of the men who are there are gazing into their beer.

"I'd go as far as to say," says Terry, "that as far as yer warm-ups go, she's pretty fucking warm, know what I mean?" He cuts his laugh short, suddenly remembering that maybe he ought to be wary. But Derek only smiles. "Yeah, Terry, I know what you mean all right."

Terry relaxes, gives Derek the benefit of his professional

little coloured piece of Derek's—Shireen, was it?—used to do. Funny bloke, Del. Still, that reminds him—it's about time they got in a new novelty act: animal stuff's back in fashion. Terry's stomach grumbles but the drink has put paid to the sharp little pain inside it for a while.

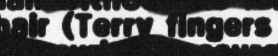

eye: "Nice titties—got a bit of a figure on her, not like that skinny bird you used to hang round with. Good skin, too, even without the warpaint."

"Young skin," says Derek. "You can't beat young skin. Got a sheen on it, a freshness."

"Yeah well, waxing poetical's one thing, long as it don't get us all into trouble."

Terry rolls the milky drink around his glass and wonders how Derek Trent does it—if he does it, mind, rather than just looking. He's always got some nice little girlie or other, not bad seeing as how he's a man without his full complement of hair (Terry fingers his own gelled curls, reassured to find they're all still there). Speaking for himself, mind

The first time Lianne hated it. She'd tried not to look down, because all she could see when she did was her thighs bulging over the top of her fishnets. She did the steps she'd practised and tried to pretend she was back home in her bedroom dancing about to make Kurt giggle. But something about that was wrong—it gave her a nasty feeling in the back of her mouth, like that time when Derek had taken all those photos of her, and somehow or other Kurt's purple dinosaur had found its way into half the bloody pictures. And the nasty feeling made her get out of sync with the music so that well before the end she had nothing left to take off. No-one booed, but no-one much clapped either. And when she was making a run for the dressing room she heard that Anita woman spew out some comment about "fucking amateurs".

Lianne had nearly gone straight home after the first show, but she'd promised Derek. And besides, it was cash in hand, wasn't it, and she

you, he'd not be too happy to let a load of blokes get an eyeful of some bird of his, let alone watch her stick the end of some moth-eaten reptile up her whosit like what that wouldn't get paid at all if she walked away, and walking away was one thing, but where the fuck did she think she was going to go? Anyhow, things are better now, she feels almost like a pro.

"Listen you silly bitch," Anita had said, "don't go anywhere while you're out there, don't go off in some daydream, stay with the show. All those men are at your feet, goggling at you, think about that—just think about it, honey."

And it works, too, in a funny way. Not that Lianne likes thinking about herself, or about her body, or about stuff like that. But she hasn't been the centre of attention like this since, ooh, that Sunday school nativity play when she was who knows how old—and Mum had soon put a stop to that. Anita says Lianne has lovely assets, beautiful skin. Anita tells her to remember who it is out there who's paying, and who it is on stage who's getting paid. Anita says think about what that means, honey.

Anita isn't so bad, really. All you have to do is ask her advice and listen like you want to know, and she'll be nice enough.

Tonight, Anita says, "You're hands are a fucking disgrace, honey," when Lianne peels off her two silver gloves in the corner of the toilets that Terry calls the dressing room. Lianne looks down. Her left wrist is much better, now the scalded patch has wrinkled and shrunk like it's grown old without the rest of her, but it's started to split open and underneath it she can see fresh pink newborn baby skin.

"I went to get the kettle and I wasn't looking-" she says. "Stupid but—"

"I mean, just look at your fingers," says Anita.

She holds up her own hands: at the end of each soft plump finger is a shiny pink spike.

Lianne studies them admiringly. "They're like..." she gropes for the right word. "Weapons."

"They are lethal fucking weapons, girlie," says Terry, putting his head round the door without bothering to knock. "Believe me. I know."

Anita laughs. She won't lower herself to talk to Terry when he's like this.

"In your own time, milady," Terry says. "Just to remind you they're out there gagging for a glimpse of ye lovely face. Or yer lovely something." Anita pushes past him with her angular elbows, making her way towards the stage, not giving a shit.

Terry strokes his stomach and watches Lianne rub the glitter off her body. He won't use language in

front of the birds, but he'd like to tell Lianne a thing or two and he can't think of the right polite words. She looks up and sees him in the mirror, waiting there by the door. For some reason he's embarrassed by her eyes; he nods, ducks out of the room. Still, there's always Friday night.

In the taxi Lianne picks at the skin on her wrist, pulling away the shrivelled bits. She'd thought Derek was going to take her home every night, but after the first couple of times he didn't show. She isn't worried about it; she knows he has things to do. And it's not as if the taxi costs her: Mr Harkness fixed it up at a special price and he takes it out her wages.

Something made of ice slithers down Lianne's spine. She makes herself open the door. Kurt's sitting on the floor, his face bright red and striped with tears. She grabs him, Ignoring the puke on his pyjamas, and stares at him as if she hopes the answer to the mystery will shine through his tiny fragile skull.

"Mel! Melanie! You all right?" There's no-one in the sitting room. "Melanie!" Lianne's almost screaming now herself. Kurt looks set to burst into tears again. There's no-one in the bedroom. Lianne sits on the bed and rocks him. She tries not to shake.

She thinks she must be imagining it when she comes along the walkway, but no, it's definitely Kurt screaming. Poor Mel, if he's been at it half the night.

By the time she gets to the flat the noise has stopped, and there aren't any lights on.

Wednesday is Mum's afternoon down the clinic. Lianne goes round with the idea in her head that she's going to sit and wait for Melanie to get in from school and then she's going to grab her by the hair and slap her smirking little gob.

She gets there at half-three and

Melanie's home already. She's not sick but she's in the bedroom—Mum's bedroom. At first Lianne can't work it

ks icy and the bre
right rhough her

d told her they'd h
gs clipped. There

out, why Mel's stretched out across the bed like that with her uniform pushed up and stupid white socks on and her knickers round her ankles, showing her fat arse to the dressing-table mirror. Then the door swings back into something soft and Derek goes "Ow."

Melanie twists her neck to see what's going on even as she strains to hold the pose. Lianne's mouth hangs open, then she closes it and shoves back against the open door with all her weight. "Jesus Christ," says Derek; crash goes his Polaroid camera. "Fuck me," says Melanie and falls off the bed with a bump.

Lianne picks Kurt up from the playgroup and takes him for a long walk in the park. She makes for the lake although there's nothing in her pockets to feed the geese with. She wheels Kurt's pushchair on to the bridge and

stops, pressing her foot on the brake three or four times before it catches. There's netting there, to stop you falling over the railings. She lifts Kurt up high and shows him the black swans with their bright red bills like splashes of blood on the grey skin of the lake. "Quackwack," says Kurt. One of the swans scoops something out of the water and swallows it, its long neck snaking down and up again in one slippery motion.

Lianne shivers. The water looks icy and the breeze cuts right through her jacket. Why don't the swans fly away, she used to wonder, then Derek had told her they'd had their wings clipped. There was some story Mum used to read them a long time ago, before she went right off her trolley, about a flock of princes who turned into swans every night (or was it the other way round?) and flew off, and then in the morning they shed their skins and turned back into princes again. This starts to seem all wrong, thinking about it, because surely birds don't do that. Lianne wishes she could remember the story properly, so she could tell it to Kurt. Maybe he wouldn't enjoy it, though; the stories they do at the playgroup are about fat harmless children and funny witches who cast the wrong spells.

Lianne puts Kurt down again; he's getting to be a heavy little bugger. "Mumma," he says, excited; he's noticed her fingernails.

"Like them?" she asks. "Pretty, aren't they?"

He clutches at her fingers with his chubby hand. "Careful, pet," she warns him, too late. He bursts into tears: Lianne's new claws are sharp.

Terry checks his belly, but though it's been playing up tonight, he's sure the gurgling came from one of the cubicles. "What's that noise?"

"The plumbing," Anita says, dusting tan powder over her shoulders and down across her neat breasts.

Terry rubs his belly again.

"Fuck off and leave us be," Anita tells him. "I'm an artiste, and I need peace and quiet and all that bollocks."

"An ar-teeste," says Terry. "That's a good one." Must be a joke there, he thinks, on the lines of "arse'n'tits, more like". Still, he doesn't chance it. He doesn't want to upset Anita—not on a Friday, when all the stagnight boys are out there baying for her.

Even after Terry's gone, though, Anita is still pissed off; it's all Lianne's fault. "Kurt's a good boy," Lianne had said, "He won't make a sound, I promise."

"He'd better not," Anita had said. "If Terry finds a baby here, there'll be trouble."

When she's sure that Terry's gone, Anita opens the door with the out-of-order sign on it and checks. The kid's still strapped in his pushchair with a fist in his mouth. He looks at her with wide eyes like an animal's.

"Shut your fucking face," says Anita, not too unkindly, and tries a smile. "Mummy's coming soon." And that's no lie, she thinks with relief, hearing Lianne's music winding up to its climax. She gives Kurt a little wave and shuts the door on him, and crosses her fingers.

On stage, Lianne is on top of it all. She tweaks a small gold star off one of her nipples and sends it sparkling up into the air; ten or twenty sweaty men scramble for it, punching each other for a little piece of her. She could stay there in the spotlight all night and nothing else would matter. Except she can't stay there all night. She rotates her hips ever so carefully, and rakes narrow paths through her pubic hair with her new fingernails, parting the shiny pink lips of her cunt the way Anita taught her, like she's showing them the great secret, the source of it all. And, for a moment or two, she really believes it.

Sooner or later, the record ends. It takes Terry, Fat Johnno and Dil the Dog to keep them in line. "Get off!" shouts Terry, louder than Lianne's ever heard him. "Now!"

Lianne's about to ask Anita how things have been, but she can see from her face that she's not happy.

"Sorry," she says. Anita gives her the evil eye and leaves for the stage, without saying anything. Lianne looks in on Kurt. He's asleep, at least. His purple dinosaur has fallen on the floor and it's lying in a puddle of stuff, but she can put it in the wash.

She sits down and looks in the mirror. A light bulb goes pop. That's fair enough, she feels, it suits her all right, the semi-darkness. A few seconds ago she was triumphant, but now her eyes have taken on a dull sheen like a pair of flat stones. In the glow from the streetlight, her glittering skin turns to scales. She takes a towel to her arms and watches the glitter flake off in brittle pieces. If she rubs hard enough, maybe all of her skin will come off like a snake's, and she can step out of it and walk away, clean, new, terrifying.

Asleep in his pushchair Kurt dreams about red swans with black claws, about black swans with red claws, about things which are shining and wet and silent. He wants to touch them, but they're keeping their distance.

"Lianne, love," Terry calls. The door has stuck, somehow. He knocks. "It's me, Terry. You got to open this. Fire regulations." He may be imagining it, but he's got it into his head that she's keeping someone in there with her. He thinks about some wanker running his fat fingers over Lianne's lovely young skin. Some fucking punter's got no right to do that, not on his premises.

"Won't be long," Lianne says. "I'm changing."

The floor is covered with sparkling fragments of Lianne; slivers of hair lie in the sink. Her underskin is tender and pink, but it's not enough.

She looks at her fingernails, honed and ready.

"You know me, I don't mind," says Terry. He pushes the door. He hears something that sounds like ripping. She'll have to pay if anything happens to the costumes.

At first it hurts a little, because

she's not quite brave enough. Her nails have scored narrow red lines on her forearms, and the surface throbs with pain. She hears Kurt's sleepy breathing. Her new pink skin is itching. She closes her eyes and scratches, properly this time; she punctures the skin and begins to peel it back. The pain is unbearable but she doesn't scream.

Terry nearly trips over in the darkness as the door swings open. Then he sees her, sitting by the mirror.

"Lianne," he begins.

She turns to look at him.

Her eyes are cold as a reptile's, but that's not what he notices. She's...wet? Shining in the neon. Like a well-oiled... No, it's not that.

She's. It's...

w muscle tendons ins, nerve cells immering throbbing

..like something out of a medical book) It's not real: it can't be—It can't be a live thing but It's standing up   (throbbing)   and there's a hole where the   mouth should be. It's moving and it smells of... ....mm............   (don't think it... ....mmnm ::::::   —meat.

"You like my skin, don't you, Terry?" it says. "Here, have it if you want."

It holds up a tattered thing that

is warm and wet against his face.

He wants to run away but his guts won't let him. He heaves and retches. Six brandy Alexanders, two pints of lager, a pile of mashed potato and a packet and a half of Rennies swim back up his gullet and fight to get out. He vomits until there's nothing left but yellow bile. And then the blood comes.

The pain has left Lianne; it floats in the   room   for   a   second,   a shimmering cloud, then dissolves into the chill night air. Above the club's stale smells of puke and smoke and sweat and piss rises the healthy stench of a butcher's counter. Her own fresh flesh.

When Anita comes offstage she finds Terry in the dressing room lying in a pool—a fucking lake, more like—of something disgusting. It looks as if his stomach's turned itself inside out. She holds her nose and accidentally treads on his hand with the high heel of her gilt sandal. He doesn't make a squawk when she feels in his jacket pocket for her wages.

Kurt wraps his arms around Lianne's neck and she carries him light as a swan's feather, into the darkness. He burrows his fingers into the gaps between her sinews; he sucks and his mouth fills with something warm and salt. "There, there, darling," she says, and holds him tight against the slow steady beat of her heart

TEEN LITE

She looks like a supermodel, a thin unhealthy junkie lookalike. Her lips speak of mystery and sex without even moving.

He is a low-life muppet with a noisy moped. An attractive eighteen year old runaway living temporarily with a vicious JesusFreak bike gang.

Her cheap wig is askew when she collects the brick-shaped package he's been asked to deliver to a child's swing in the park. As she goes she is smiling and her body is sort of floating backwards and forwards as if all the parts of it are only loosely connected and she isn't really walking on the ground.

Alistair Gentry

She likes him for the dense, percussive excitement which he provides. He likes her because she's so well-spoken and has a collection of frightening and ominous Klaus Barbie dolls and Action Mengeles.

One of his home-recorded tapes 'Techno Various' has inexplicably been altered, replaced in part by sounds resembling Morse code. He has played the tape before on countless occasions. One side of the tape is pure dance music. The other side now contains techno and essential but indecipherable information in code.

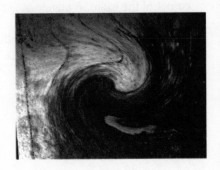

Her new telephone re-Oedipalises her. She calls her daddy every day. He is an architect and will not answer, but a demonic voice leaves complex messages on her answerphone. Sophisticated analysis of the tape shows that it begins with the words I hate you. She wills him to pick up pick up pick up as she twists a spiral umbilicus around her fingers. He never does.

The party is a dull and pointless exercise in content-free social exchanges. She is bored and takes quite a few pills. Valium or Ecstasy, Temazepam or Mogadon, she forgets which. Right then he takes her arms and leads her off into a corner of the room. A man in a bathing suit and his fashionable Japanese girlfriend move aside and there on the PC monitor is his face. She tries to close his mouth by dragging the cursor to lift his jaw. She goes too far and his lower lip sails up and penetrates his nose, making a disgusting but not entirely unfamiliar grimace.

The next day she grinds her teeth a lot and she sits in the living room feeling crazed and frightened.

Saturday they watch television and read supermarket novels. Sunday he buries her up to her neck in his back garden, making her feel
    a) stupid
      b) erotic and
        c) claustrophobic.
         Wednesday she sees five enormous birds resembling pterodactyls, with leathery bodies and wings, wheeling over the house like vultures. They stay up all night drinking and bullshitting one another. It all begins to feel so significant.

They have long and unflinching discussions about (amongst other things):

Chaos theory and chaos practice;
Viruses and decay;
Today's global politico-corporate power structure;
What happens when your sexual impulses spin out of control;
How one would go about making a citizen's arrest (and whether one can do so without getting one's face kicked in);
How much it costs to die;
The true nature of love;
Can you really drink your own pee?

They systematically listen to each other's vinyl. She tells him how she never liked ambient music until somebody told her that *ambienté* is Mexican slang for gay.

A large quantity of cash and personal items is missing from her flat. For several days afterwards lights are seen and a shadowy figure moves about as she tries to sleep. Yet each time the police are called no-one is found. They live together for two weeks, then the haunting stops.

—I don't even know what Shiatsu is. Will a medium vigorous vibration do, babe?

—You're all glitter on the edges and profoundly stupid in the middle.
(*Pause*)
—Did you make that one up yourself?

He reassures himself that he doesn't need the very best. He is perfectly happy with something that is reasonably adequate. She has been dabbling in pornography. He finds a poorly focused Hi-8 stag film featuring her and an arcane sect of Satanists. It bears a sticker saying YOU MUST BE 18 YEARS OLD TO PURCHASE THIS OR YOU WILL GROW UP TO BE A DEPRAVED SEX MURDERER.

She anticipates the incriminations and recriminations by writing crude insults on her arms in felt tip. Her intention is ironic, but instead she gives the impression of someone hanging on by her acrylic fingernails. He desperately hopes that her bizarre behaviour is a nightmare. It isn't.

—My God. The world's insane. We're contemplating madness.
(*Apropos of nothing.*)
He reacts like your mum reading a book, when you show her your drawing and her x-ray vision enables her to appraise your drawing without looking up from her book.

—Our relationship is too intellectual. Too abstract. Too contained. Too noisy. I find it difficult to see how anyone could have been fooled by this dwarfed, desiccated pastiche of a relationship. But we were fooled. I've had it up to here with this entropy business.
—Explain yourself, woman.
—*I am ranting and you don't explain rants.*

They float away from each other like a double helix broken into two single strands of nucleotides. They become something new by accumulating all the things they can no longer be.

He keeps on calling her, even though she's told him on several occasions to please be finished with her. His grammar is often bad; he uses (for example) 'obsolete' as a verb. He suggests deviant sexual conduct in a violent context. After these scenes they are both trembly and smoke cigarettes.

Marlboro Lights for her, Silk Cut 100s for him.

He waits for her outside her flat one night. A small hand-held sprayer, similar to a pepper or mace canister, unloads a 7olb blast of bright green foam dye into his face. It helps no end when she has to pick him out of a police line-up a week later. Crying, she tells herself, doesn't make any sense in an age of instantaneous global communication and babies whelped in petri dishes. And call me Winston Smith if you like, she thinks, but the idea of wiring up the whole world isn't something which gives me comfort.

He dies under strange circumstances. Somebody tells her that he was in a fight over a rent boy. His neighbour says that he was discovered as a pile of ashes in the shower, his skull shrunken to the size of a baseball. He had come into her world as a question mark, and is delivered in a bin bag to the morgue with a question mark. A Post-It note is found requesting that he be sewn into a canvas shroud with the last stitch piercing the gristle between the nostrils, and committed to the deep. This being rather impractical, he is cremated. Like he needs it.

With hindsight she realises that she had always seen the zipper up the back of that monster guy. And she thought she had killed all the Space Invaders. She grew up, bought her own television set and forgot all about them.
But they faxed her the scary news about herself from the past.

She puts on some *ambienté* music and shakes rhythmically all night.

THE SNiPER
SiMON
MiLES

i am a sniper.
Day after day i lie alone on my hill, pointing my rifle at a village in the valley.
i concentrate on the path to the east of the school.
it is here that the villagers come out into the open to fetch water from the well.
in the past month i have wounded six villagers, and killed two.
i have also fallen in love with a village girl.
Although i cannot see her perfectly through my sights, i think she is probably beautiful.

This love does not feel unreasonable to me. After all, it is possible to hate strangers from a distance. How else could I fire my rifle? So why can I not love from a distance as well?

Indeed, I suggest that this type of hate and this type of love, detached as they are by the distance between their objects and I, have a purity denied to the complicated world of personal relationships. They are instead inspired by greater...principles.

The hate is based not merely on my feelings, but my feelings about my parents' feelings, about their parents' feelings--about past slaughter-- which I feel a duty to prevent from ever happening again. I kill only to stop killing.

My love is also inspired by duty--the duty to express, through love, my respect for and devotion to beauty. For it is beauty after all, in all its forms, that we are fighting to protect.

These are the principles which keep me sane, as i lie on my hill, day after day.

I call the girl I love Layali because I like the
sound.

It reminds me of the wind blowing through the
grass as I lie and watch her. She's the only one who
dares walk towards the well. She flirts with me. She
knows I'm here--guiding her within my sights from
left to right with empty pail, and from right to
left with full pail back.

I imagine that the circle of my sights defines a
forcefield, in which she is completely safe, as long
as I can keep her there.

I sometimes shoot at her, but not to kill her. I
shoot to make her move for me. For example: She may
be wearing a loose cotton dress, gathered at the
waist so the fabric billows imprecisely at her chest.
If I shoot just behind her, an inch or so above the
small of her back, she has to arch it, flinging her
arms up in the air, and forcing the shape of her
breasts out against the cotton for me.

Or, by aiming just above her head, I can make
her suddenly bend at the waist--turning straight
lines into curves for my imagination.

She is a matador to my precise love, who throws
her arms above her head and reels on her tiny heels,
her long black flailing hair ripping at the dusty
air, while my bullet sails towards the woods.

Sometimes water slops from her pail, and
splashes in the dust, making her angry. She will
stop dancing, catch the light with her eyes and fire
it back up here at me.

She has 'hit' me like
this, with her eyes, seven
times.
I could have killed her seven
times. We are well matched,
my love and I.

I have always loved nature. In the
past, the weight of my fast boots has made many of
its smaller inhabitants flee in panic, splitting
and dividing beneath my heels. But now, keeping as
still as I do on my hill, I have become as
familiar to them as the land itself--part of their
territory, over which they stride with tiny steps,
going about their business, making and protecting
their homes.

Even the shock of gunshot fails to arouse
more than a brief hiccough in their rhythm. It's
surprising what insects, as well as humans, will
get used to.

I have even known ants to walk out along the
oiled barrel of my gun, and to disappear up inside
it. One day an unfortunate ant failed to crawl out
before I had pressed the trigger, and had to hold
onto a bullet for dear life while it shot down
into the valley and into the body of an old man.

Incredibly the ant managed to escape from the
wound and find its way back up
the hill. I know this,
because I saw it
arrive, a little worse
for wear, but its
little antennae still
waving excitedly in
anticipation of
telling its friends of
its adventure.

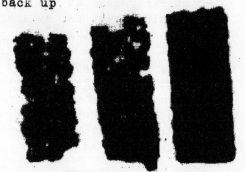

*Last night Layali came to
me in a dream, barefoot from the village,
pirouetting past my sights through the moonlight
with a pail from the well that spilt blood in the
dust of the path. Her arm raised to wave, and a
hand eclipsed the moon, and came down on my face.*

*She opened my mouth, and slid my rifle across
my teeth, down into my belly.*

*Above me the stars were like distant bombs
being dropped on darkness, exploding as Layali's
eyes filled with dirty water that burst like a
drain over cheeks which began to swell--until her*

mouth erupted, in a gush of fat and frightened
ants that struggled free of her saliva to crawl
all over me. And I grabbed at the gun to shoot
her, to stop this foul flood, but it was rammed
inside my own throat, and my finger trembled on
the trigger.

I woke up clutching my rifle as if I were a
child and the rifle were my mother.

Today I was told
that our army plans
to take over the
villages in the
valley.

I know what
this means. First
we shell the
village. Then
tanks roll in
from the west,
with infantry
made up of the
army, and
irregulars.

If things
go well, the
men will be
put on busses
to the camps
behind our
lines,
leaving the
women, the old, and children to join the refugee
route up north. But things don't always go well.
Fear, exhaustion, and anger sometimes take
control. Layali is young and very beautiful.
Beauty sometimes makes people behave in ugly ways.

Crimes like these are just the frothy head on
war--not part of the real campaign--an unavoidable
rather than a necessary evil.

I know that. And yet I feel physically sick,
with a mind full of pictures, in which
Layali...What can I do?

My mind grows confused and unreliable --like my trigger finger. I can't even rely on myself to miss her anymore. Maybe I should kill her--wait for a smile and pin her to it forever.

Or maybe, by shooting at her feet, I could force her backwards from the well and into the river. The current would carry her to the gorge behind our lines, where I could meet her in the rushes.

Or I could ask my friends, the ants, to bear her up to me at night upon their million backs.

The attack on the village took place yesterday. i watched from the hill.

Tiny people running in all directions, like molecules under heat. Feet kicking up the dust. A bloody rodeo.

When it was over, just slow smoke and a return to birdsong, I went down into the valley for the first

time. It felt like sacrilege. The village had been
a distant place--a doll's house voodoo altar for
me to stick my bullets into.

   I had to see Layali again, to feel sane
again. The violence of the attack had shocked me.
I'd been surprised by the scale of the horror in
relation to the size of the people. Layali's
beauty would remind me of sanctity, and sanctity
would remind me of duty, and duty would remind me
of why I have to be here, fighting this fucking
righteous war.
   Layali's beauty would make sense of
everything again.

I found her with the other women, in the school.
Awkward bodies splayed and ripped, like burst
mattresses. She was on her back by the blackboard.
Her ankles were tied to her wrists, forcing her
bent legs to fall open into the shape of a
diamond, bloodied at one apex. Her mouth was
full of chalk.
      I walked up to her and bent over to
      look into her eyes. After all those months
      I was so close I could touch her. But I
      didn't. Her eyes were dark. No sun in
      them to fire at me like on those
         happy afternoons when I'd held her
         in my sights. But there was
         enough light in the room
         to see her
         perfectly.
            And it was
            then that I
            realised how
            wrong I'd
            been--how
            fucking wrong
            I'd been all
            along. She was
            not beautiful
            after all.

Simon Miles, a freelance
journalist, wrote The Sniper
after a trip to Bosnia to write
about rape babies.

SKIN UP with PULP MULTIBUY

Order any 3 *PULP Faction* books
and receive a *free* copy of *SKIN* (while stocks last).

I enclose a cheque payable to *PULP Faction* for:

- [ ] £18.00 Any 3 titles (specify) ....
....plus a *free* copy of SKIN.
- [ ] £5.99 SKIN
- [ ] £6.99 TECHNOPAGAN
- [ ] £6.99 THE LIVING ROOM
- [ ] £6.99 FISSION
- [ ] £6.99 RANDOM FACTOR

- [ ] Please include submission details
for future Pulp Faction titles.

Name ....
Address ....
Postcode ....

***Return to:* Pulp Faction, BooksDirect, 60 Alexander Road, London, N19 3PQ.**
Books delivered post-free to any UK address.
Orders from outside the UK, add £1.50 p&p per book or £4 per multibuy.
Credit card orders on: 0500 418 419 (24hr service).